VOYAGE OF DEATH & DESIRE

Vampires of Charleston
Book 1

Madalyn Rae

This book is dedicated to vampire lovers everywhere. Thank you for biting... (see what I did there?)

content warning

As with most vampire stories, there is quite a bit of violence and torture. Mentions of sexual abuse, child abuse, drug use, and physical abuse, along with many mentions of blood and death, are scattered throughout the book.

leaving home

STANDING in the middle of our small cottage, I hold all of my earthly possessions inside the worn fabric of my filthy apron. Being the oldest of nine children, I'm in charge of the girls, while my brother, Charles, oversees the boys.

"Elsbeth, make sure the girls have all their belongings," Mama says as she swaddles the baby and places it in the bog. The smallest member of our family hasn't received a name yet. After losing three young babies, Mama refuses to name them until they make it through the unforgiving Scottish winter.

I look into the face of the baby boy she's holding close. I've nicknamed him Aaron, after my father. Black circles underline his wide eyes, and he's smaller than he should be at five months old. "Elsbeth, did ya hear me?"

"Aye. Sorry, Mum." I turn toward the three girls

standing in front of me. Each holds a small bundle similar to mine. "You three have all your things?"

Each girl nods. My sisters are young. After I was born, there seemed to be a time when Mama couldn't have anything but boys. The three-, five-, and six-year-old girls stare at me, wide-eyed and terrified.

"Charles, how about the boys?" she asks my brother.

"We're good," he answers.

"Good. Let's go." Mama takes a deep breath before leading us away from the cottage for the last time.

The walk to the marina is long and cold as the winter winds have already begun to blow. The sun is sinking lower in the sky as we slowly make our way toward town. "Elsbeth, make sure the girls keep up," she demands.

I turn, finding the youngest of my sisters lagging. The fabric that's tied around her feet has begun to tear, and her toes are sticking out. The one pair of shoes the girls share is too big for her right now, meaning she's wearing a flour sack wrapped around her feet.

"Bonnie, keep up."

"I can't," she cries. "My feet aren't working."

I turn around and pick her up, pulling her to my side. She barely weighs anything. She sniffs deeply and sinks her face into my shoulder. "Thank you, Elsie."

In the distance, I see the tops of large sails, letting me know we're close. I sigh in relief. Truthfully, my feet hurt, too, and with the added weight of Bonnie, the walk has gotten harder.

We enter the outskirts of the village, catching the stares of strangers and people we've known all our lives. Each judges us as we pass. Some are whispering, telling stories of why we're leaving. Most don't know the truth...only what they believe to be the truth.

"Keep up," Mama warns from in front.

"Wow," Bonnie whispers over my shoulder. "Is that what we're riding on to America?"

"That's it. Stay quiet now," I warn as we approach. Men of all different shapes and sizes stop what they're doing and stare at the ten of us as we approach.

An older man with a round belly steps forward first. "What can I help you with, milady?" The crowd around him erupts into laughter at his formal greeting for my mother.

She pulls a paper from her bosom. "My children and I have paid for passage to America."

The man looks at the paper, turning it in several different directions. "Is that what this says?"

"It is," Mama answers. "My name is Eleanor Abernathy, and these are my children."

"*Your* children?" the man asks. "You look too young to have all these children. Where's your husband?" He turns toward the line behind her. We're standing as we always do, in order of height.

"Dead," she answers plainly.

"I'm sorry to hear that, ma'am." His words are monotone and flat.

Even though Charles is a year younger than me, he's been taller than me for years, which means he's at the head of the line, directly behind Mama. The man takes in my brother's features, giving me an uncomfortable feeling. When he moves closer to me, he stops. "Aren't you a lovely one?" Picking up a piece of my dark hair, he rubs it between his fingers. "How old are you, dearie?"

"Nineteen," I answer truthfully.

"Nineteen and no husband? How is someone so lovely not married with a few wee bairns?"

I stare at the giant in front of me, refusing to answer. He has no business knowing why I've been scorned and considered unfit for marriage, and no reason to know that I'm the cause of my family being forced to leave Scotland and my father's death. I stare at the beast of a man in front of me, daring him to ask again. He lets go of my hair and rubs a thick finger across my cheek before continuing down the line, assessing each of my siblings as he passes.

"Go ahead then." He shakes the ticket Mama gave him in the air, shooing us toward the awaiting vessel. A few of the men standing around whistle as we board. I move to the back of the line, feeling the need to protect the smallest members of my family.

The ship we board is large and made of wood with three sets of extra-large sails on top. "Follow me to your quarters," the large man says as he leads us through a narrow door behind the helm.

The smell of urine and other excrement hits me the moment the door opens. He opens an even smaller door on the side of the hallway and issues a warning to someone inside. "Get out!" he shouts, slamming the door open.

A young girl, not much older than me, runs past with the top part of her dress hanging open.

"Here you go, milady." He motions toward the now empty space. "Your room."

Mama steps into the room. "Is this for *all* of us?" she asks.

"I'm afraid it's all we can spare."

"It will do then," she answers.

The rest of us enter the small room, finding a wooden platform, a brass pot that is one of the sources of the smell, and a small wooden chair. The room is barely big enough for one, let alone ten.

"We set sail in an hour," the man bellows before leaving us alone in the room.

Mama sighs and straightens her skirt. "Well, we'll just make this our home for the next few weeks." She looks me in the eyes. "We can do anything we set our minds to, as long as we're together."

I nod, setting Bonnie down for the first time. My back sighs in relief. "Where are we going to sleep?" I ask, looking around the small room.

"The girls will sleep on the bed, and the boys can sleep on the floor."

For the first time today, the baby cries. His voice is weaker than usual as he whimpers for food.

"Shut that baby up," a deep voice sounds through the hallway.

She pulls him from the bog and tries to feed him. He has a hard time latching onto her breast, but thankfully manages.

I turn toward my sisters. "Why don't we get this out of here?" I nod toward the disgusting brass pot.

"Eww," Bonnie answers.

"Aye, I agree. But I'm not staying another minute with it in here. Get the door." I pick up the pot, being careful not to splash the excrement in the room. Bonnie is the only girl who follows as I head back through the narrow door onto the deck. We move quickly to the side and dump the disgusting contents into the water below.

"Oh, that stinks," Bonnie says, holding her nose. "What are they eating?"

I laugh, wondering the same thing. "I need to wash my hands. Can you take the pot back to the room?"

"Do I have to?" she asks, pursing her face into a disgusted pattern.

"Yes. I don't want to touch anything after that."

Bonnie sighs and pulls the pot closer to her. "It still smells," she groans, walking back toward the room.

I wait until she's safely inside before looking for

somewhere to wash. Most of the men on board are busy preparing to set sail. In the back of the ship behind the helm is a bucket of what appears to be clean water. At least I can see the bottom of the bucket. That's as clean as I can expect at this moment. Bending down, I plunge my hands into the coldness, wiping the human excrement from my palms. I rub my hands together until the skin begins to feel raw. Satisfied that they're as clean as they'll get, I wipe the water onto the worn fabric of my apron.

Standing, I turn, finding myself facing a man wearing a blue velvet waistcoat. "Did you just wash your hands in my drinking water?" he asks, staring down at me. He's the kind of man we don't have around the village. Tall, handsome, and clean.

I fight the butterflies swarming in my stomach and square my shoulders before making eye contact with him. "Yes?" I point at the bucket. "It was just sitting there, and I needed a place to wash up."

"Who are you?" he asks.

"Elsbeth Abernathy."

"Why are you here, *Elsbeth Abernathy?*"

"My...my family is on board. We're going to Charles Town."

He looks behind me. "Your family? Where are they?"

I point toward the narrow door. "They're in one of the staterooms. My mother has a copy of the ticket if you'd like to see it."

The man bows his head. "That won't be necessary,

Miss. Abernathy. I have no reason to doubt that you have paid for your passage aboard my ship."

"Your ship?"

He smiles, lifting one side of his mouth higher than the other and bringing the butterflies to a full-fledged attack. "Aye." He holds out a large hand, taking mine and lifting it to his lips. "Captain Hawthorne Rex at your service."

"Captain?"

"Aye. Welcome aboard, Miss. Abernathy. I'm sure we will be seeing more of each other." He turns toward the bucket of now defiled water. "If you'll excuse me, it seems I need to acquire fresh water for our trip."

"I apologize. I didn't know who to ask."

"Don't give it another thought." He picks up the bucket, throwing the dirty water overboard. "We'll be departing soon. It might be better for you to be with your family."

I bow slightly and turn toward the door. "Miss. Abernathy?" he calls.

"Aye?"

"If you have any problems, please let me know immediately." He raises his voice as he continues. "I provide safe passage for women and children. Any man who questions that service or has other ideas in mind will answer to me."

"Thank you, Captain." I bow once more before entering the narrow door.

"Everything okay?" Mama asks as I enter the small room.

"Aye. It took a while to find somewhere to clean my hands." I leave out the part about meeting the captain.

"Good. Help me get the room set up."

I look around the room. "What is there to set up?"

"I'm not letting my children sleep on this filthy floor. Take off your apron, and use it as a broom."

"My apron?"

"Aye. It's all we have." She takes off hers, folding it neatly and wiping the platform free of things I don't want to know about while I do the same to the floor. My sisters copy our movements and work alongside Mama to clean the sleeping area. It doesn't take long before the room is less dirty than before.

A loud whistle sounds from outside. "What's that about?" Mama asks.

I shrug. "Maybe the ship is about to depart."

"Go find out," she demands.

I don't question her and head back to the deck of the ship. The sun is now completely set, and a full moon has taken its place. The light of the moon casts an eerie glow across the bow and the surrounding land.

The man I met earlier, Captain Rex, is behind the helm, while the large man who showed us to our room is barking orders at the crew. I watch in awe as the sails are turned and a large anchor is pulled out of the sea below. The men work in tandem, reminding me of the oxen Daddy used to plow our land.

The perfectly choreographed display is awe-inspiring to watch. Within minutes, the ship separates from the wooden dock and begins moving toward the sea. It doesn't take long before the shadows of the land begin to shrink.

"What are you doing out here, little lady?" The large man from earlier is suddenly in front of me.

"I was curious what the whistle was about."

He lifts the same strand of hair from earlier and brings it to his nose. "You like whistles, do ya?" He smiles, showing the one remaining tooth in his mouth. I refuse to answer but keep my eyes on his. "I can show you a whis..." The man is pulled away from our conversation and shoved against a wall behind the helm.

"What are you doing, Smith?" Captain Rex asks. His arm is shoved across the large man's neck as he presses it into his throat.

"Nothing, sir. Just checking on the young lady." His words are distressed as he fights to speak. "She seemed scared."

"You were trying to protect her?" the captain continues.

"Of course, sir. I wouldn't want any member of the crew to try to take advantage of her."

The scene in front of me is terrifying, but I refuse to retreat into the room with my family. "Is he telling the truth, Miss Abernathy?" Captain Rex asks.

The large man pushed against the wall begs me

with his eyes. I sigh before answering. "Yes. Mr. Smith was checking on my safety."

Smith's eyes close as he realizes the lie I told for him. Captain Rex releases his hold, allowing the man to breathe again. "Don't concern yourself with her *safety* again. Do I make myself clear?"

"Yes, sir," Smith answers, moving quickly to the front of the ship.

The captain turns toward me. "Go inside, now."

I stare at the large man, unsure how to respond. Instead of arguing, I return to the room holding my family. Once inside, Charles shoves the only piece of furniture, a small chair, against the door as a makeshift door lock. Truthfully, it's useless against anything larger than a fly, but I keep that to myself. He positions himself next to the chair with his back against the door, blocking it with his weight.

Since Daddy died, Charles has taken on the responsibility for the family. He's only seventeen but feels like it's his job to take care of all of us. Instead of climbing on top of the too small platform alongside my sisters and mother, I slide beside him, helping him block the entrance.

"Are you okay?" I whisper.

"Do you want the truth?" He leans his shoulder into mine. I don't answer. Instead, I wrap my arm through his and pull him close.

Charles is taller than me, but his features are still

young. His dark hair is the same color as mine, but where he has Daddy's blue eyes, mine are green.

"You know our well-being isn't your responsibility, right? You don't have to take all of that on your shoulders."

"I know." His voice is barely loud enough to hear.

"Mama has a job waiting for her when we get to Charles Town, and I'm sure I can get one when we arrive. I can help."

He turns toward me. "What if you have a *spell* while you're away from Mama?"

"Then I'll have a spell. I'll be okay. I'm always okay."

"Elsie, you can't take that chance. You know what happened..." Charles doesn't finish his sentence.

"I know. But that was different." I lay my head on his shoulder. "Get some sleep. I have a feeling we're going to need it."

His breathing slows down quickly and joins the symphony of snores coming from the rest of our family. The rocking of the ship, combined with the heat of the room, lulls me into a deep sleep quicker than intended.

voices in the night

"BETHIE, ARE YOU ALL RIGHT?" *I turn, finding my father sitting next to me. He's wearing the same clothes as the last time I saw him.*

"Daddy?" I whisper. "How are you here?"

His warm smile brings tears to my eyes. "I'm always here, Bethie." He uses the nickname he gave me as an infant. "Are ya healthy?"

The tears escape, running down my cheeks. "I am. Daddy, I'm sorry. I didn't mean…"

"I know, Bethie," he answers. "I know, my love."

"Elsbeth!" Charles's voice echoes in my ear. "Something's wrong!"

It takes a few minutes to get my bearings and leave the dream. "Charles? What are you talking about?"

"Bertram's breathing weird. I don't know what to do."

I turn toward my youngest brother, realizing his

head is on Charles's lap. His breathing is shallow, he's soaking wet, and his skin is pale. "When was the last time he ate?" I ask.

Charles shrugs. "I don't know. I don't even know the last time I ate."

"He needs food and water. I've seen him like this before." An older woman in the village once told my mother that he had a sugar sickness. When he was a baby, he would have attacks often. As he grew, they became less frequent. I stand, moving toward the door.

"Where are you going?"

"To find food." I look up, realizing Mama and the rest of our family are still sleeping. "I'll be back soon."

"I'll go," Charles moves to stand.

"No. I'm smaller and will blend into the shadows. Stay with Bert."

He nods. "Hurry."

The sounds of snoring echo through the hallway as I make my way toward the main deck. I'm relieved to find it empty. The full moon illuminates the wooden floorboards as the waves lap gently against the sides of the ship. I take a minute to appreciate the beauty in front of me. I've lived near the sea my entire life, but this is the first time I've been surrounded by nothing but water.

Laughter behind me draws my attention back to the present. "Food for Bertram," I remind myself.

Light shines onto the deck from an open window not far from the helm. I move closer, hearing what sounds like a game of some sort between a group of men. "Play the damn card, Cap'n," a deep voice bellows. "We all know it ain't nothin' good." Loud laughter echoes through the room.

The sound of something slapping against wood brings a roar of laughter from the crowd inside. "Oh, look," a voice I recognize from earlier says. "I did have a good hand." The men continue laughing as the sound of coins being moved around follows. "Get some rest, gentlemen. Something tells me this is going to be a long trip."

The door opens, giving me enough time to slide into the shadows and watch as a small handful of men exit the room. Most appear drunk and are too busy trying to walk upright to notice me.

I wait until the men are no longer in sight before moving toward the still opened door. A small candelabra is glowing, filling the room with light. In the corner is what I need. What looks like a half-eaten loaf of bread is sitting next to an apple and orange. My stomach growls at the sight.

I'm not sure where Captain Rex went, but the room is empty. I move as quietly as possible inside and straight to the table holding the food. A large napkin sits near the bread. I shove the apple and orange into my apron pocket before wrapping what's left of the bread inside the napkin.

I turn, expecting someone to be there, and thankfully, discover the room is still empty. Moving toward the table, I find a pitcher full of liquid. I doubt it contains water, but Bertram needs something to drink.

"I didn't peg you for a heavy drinker," the voice I recognize as Captain Rex's says from behind me.

I turn, facing the large man. The coat he was wearing earlier is off, along with his shirt, revealing parts of a man I've never seen before. My eyes betray me, taking in every peak and valley of his chest, down to the waistband of the loose-fitting pants he's wearing.

"It's not for me," I answer, not sure what else to say.

"Who's it for?"

"My brother. He's ill. He needs food and drink."

Captain Rex moves into the room. "Don't give him what's in that container. Let me get you water. I have some back here." He turns, leaving me alone.

I don't know whether to run or follow. I choose neither and stay put. He's back less than a minute later with a crock full of liquid. "Here. This is clean. Is there anything else you need?"

"Food," I answer truthfully. My family is hungry and hasn't eaten in a few days."

He nods toward a box on the other side of the room. "Take what you need."

The tigereye wooden cabinet opens easily. Inside, I find an uncut loaf of bread, along with several more apples. "Are you sure?"

"Of course. I could never eat all of that. Take what

you need." I feel his eyes on my back as I take the bread and enough fruit for each child to have their own.

"Thank you, Captain."

"Please, call me Thorne."

I bow slightly. "Thank you, Thorne."

"Aye, it's my pleasure. Please feel free to get food for them anytime you need it." I stare, not sure if this is some sort of trick or genuine kindness. "If you should need anything, Miss Abernathy, please don't hesitate to ask."

"Elsbeth," I remind him. "My name is Elsbeth."

"Elsbeth," he repeats. My name flows from his lips.

"Thank you, Thorne." I turn, moving toward the door without looking back.

Back in the stateroom, I hand the loaf of bread to Charles, along with the water Thorne sent. "Help me get some of this food into Bertram. It will make him feel better."

Charles spends several minutes breaking the bread into small pieces, while I peel the skin off an orange. Manually opening Bertram's mouth, I squeeze the juice inside. Seconds later, he begins to lick his lips. "He's coming around," Charles announces.

"What's going on?" Bertram mumbles, looking around confused.

"You needed food," I answer. "Can you sit up?"

"I...I think so." He slides his back to the wall, holding onto my shoulder. "My head hurts."

"Eat this," Charles says, handing him a few pieces of bread. "See if it helps."

Bertram follows directions, closing his eyes afterward. "I'm thirsty."

"Here." Charles guides our brother's hand to the cup of water, helping him lift it to his lips. A few small sips later, his eyes close, and his breathing has returned to normal.

"How do you feel?" I ask.

"Better. Thank you."

"What's going on?" Mama's sleepy voice whispers.

Bertram shakes his head without speaking. I know without asking, he doesn't want Mama to worry. "We couldn't sleep," I answer. "We're just talking about our life in Charles Town."

Mama stares at us for a few minutes before seemingly accepting my answer. "Get some rest, Mama," Charles adds. "Everything is fine."

I don't enjoy lying to our mother, but I understand Bertram's reasoning. With Daddy's death leaving barely enough money to survive, she's been forced to move our family halfway around the world. She's under enough pressure without adding the worry of Bertram to it.

"Where'd you get food?" Bert asks. His voice sounds more like himself as he eats a few more pieces of bread.

"I found it," I lie. Technically, I did find it. Untechnically, it was given to me after I found it. "There's enough for you to eat." I hand a piece to Charles.

"Are you sure? The little ones need to eat first."

"There's plenty. Besides, I know where to find more if we need it." My mind flashes back to Captain Rex... Thorne, as he asked me to call him.

Charles takes a few bites, closing his eyes after. "God, this tastes amazing."

Bertram and Charles fall back to sleep quickly, while I sit with my back to the door, listening to the chorus of sounds created by the wooden ship. The vessel creaks and moans its way through the water, bringing comfort with its movement. With all the questions flying through my mind and the stifling heat of our stateroom, there's no way I'll be able to go back to sleep. I need fresh air and time to think.

I crack the door enough to crawl into the narrow hallway. The fresh air hits me the moment I'm outside. For the first time in a few days, I take time to breathe.

Other than a few sleeping sailors, the deck is clear of people and distractions. A gust of wind lifts the few strands of hair that escaped my hastily made bun. Moving to the head of the ship, I stand, overlooking the water below. Even with the sails down and no one at the helm, the ship continues to move slowly through the water. What if we sail off course?

I move as high as possible, giving me a full view of the dark water surrounding the ship. The full moon provides enough light to illuminate the small waves.

Breathing the clean air into my lungs is just what I need. Several breaths later, the fog that's been hiding in my head lifts slightly. "Hello," a voice whispers into the wind. I turn, finding the deck empty behind me. The hairs on my arm stand at attention.

Peering into the water below, I search for a small vessel that could be the source of the sound, finding nothing.

"You're a beautiful one," it continues. "Such lovely hair and eyes." The voice seems to be carried by the wind. I step down, moving away from the railing. "Don't go," it whispers.

Stepping backward, I move away from the edge toward the middle of the main deck. "Elsbeth, there's nothing out there. You're tired and hungry, and your imagination is getting the best of you," I say out loud, hoping to provide comfort.

"Elsbeth," the voice whispers from the sea. "What a beautiful name..."

I shuffle backward, refusing to turn my back toward the voice. Every inch of my body is on alert. This is something I don't have a name for—that terrifies me. I continue shuffling backward, working my way toward the door to the stateroom. With my back pressed against the wall, I peer into the sea, not sure if I've lost my mind, or just on the verge of it.

The door to the captain's quarters opens, revealing the man who saved my brother. He steps into the fading moonlight.

"Good morning, Captain," I whisper.

"Elsbeth, is everything okay?" He moves in front of me.

"I…I don't know. I heard…" I stop before saying more than I should.

"You heard something?"

Shaking my head. "It must have been the wind." I smooth the wrinkles on my skirt, taking a few minutes to get my thoughts together. "I'm sorry to have bothered you."

"You haven't bothered me. I was beginning my day." He steps toward the helm, unwrapping the rope holding the wheel into place. "This is my favorite time of the day. Everything feels fresh and new." He takes a deep breath, mimicking mine from earlier. "Up here, you can see the sun beginning to rise over the horizon."

"I'm sure it's lovely," I answer, unsure of where this conversation is heading.

"Join me." He reaches his hand toward me, offering to help me onto the pedestal. Refusing his help, I grab hold of the base of the wheel and pull myself to the top. Thorne chuckles at my stubbornness.

"Stand here." He steps away from the wheel, giving me space to move. I do as he suggests and am met with the first light of the morning sun.

"It is beautiful," I whisper.

"Aye. See that way?" He points north. "If you look carefully, the sun will reflect off the ice that sticks out from the sea."

"Ice?"

"Aye, icebergs. Large enough to sink a vessel of this size." He points ahead of us. "This way is America."

I turn toward my tour guide. "Have you been there before? America, I mean."

"Once, when I was a boy, but never as a Captain."

"Don't take this the wrong way, but what if you're heading in the wrong direction?"

Thorne laughs, sending chill bumps over my skin. "I have my tools." He holds up something I recognize from books.

"A sextant," I interrupt.

His eyebrows raise at my words. "Not many people know what a sextant is."

I shrug. "I read as much as possible before we left home."

"Here." He hands me the contraption that I've only read about. "Look through—"

"I know how to use it," I interrupt. Putting it to my eye, I line the mirror up with the horizon. Other than the basics of how to use it, I don't know what I'm looking at. I hand it back to him, trying not to seem obvious.

Thorne doesn't seem annoyed at what Mama calls my "independent streak." It's *one* of the reasons I've made it to nearly twenty years old without being married. In the village where we live, most girls are married or at least betrothed by thirteen or fourteen. I close my eyes, wishing the memory away.

"How is your brother?" he asks.

"Better. Thank you." Turning my head toward the rising sun, I take one last breath. "Thank you for bringing me up here. You were right. This is the most beautiful time of the day." The energy between us suddenly feels awkward, warming my cheeks and giving me a reason to escape quickly. "I need to go check on my family. Thank you again, Thorne."

"You're welcome, Elsbeth." I feel his eyes on me as I make my way to the door that leads into the sweltering stateroom that houses my family.

a meal fit for a queen

"AH, THERE YOU ARE," Mama says as I enter the room. "Everything okay?"

I smile. "I'm good. How is the baby?" I move toward the smallest member of our family. His coloring looks better than yesterday, which gives me hope.

"He seems good." She takes a small bite of the bread I brought in. "Charles says you found this food on board." She closes her eyes, relishing the flavor. "I don't want to know any details, but I'm glad you did."

I look around the room, seeing my siblings eating their fruit. Everyone looks healthier. "I think I can get more if we need it," I whisper.

"Are you being safe?" she asks.

"Aye."

Her frail hand wraps around my arm. "Thank you."

The day passes quickly. We used what remained of the water to clean the small room to the best of our ability, which means while we have a cleaner place to live for the next few weeks, I will need to ask Thorne for more water.

Each time I've passed the helm, Thorne has been standing in position at the wheel, seemingly not noticing me. I resist the urge to speak to him. For what reason, I don't know.

As the sun begins to set, I help Mama give the smaller kids a bath with water she pulled from the sea. I can't remember the last time I had a bath, and the memory makes me greedy with the desire to experience hot water surrounding my skin once again.

The sun is nearly below the horizon when I realize the main deck has emptied in the time we've been out here. My stomach rumbles, reminding me that I am most likely not the only one in my family who's hungry. "Why don't you take the children back to the room? I'll get us something to eat."

"Elsbeth..." Mama starts.

"I'll be fine. It won't take long."

From the look on her face, I can only imagine what she thinks I'm doing in exchange for nourishment. I watch her take my siblings inside. Charles stays behind, propping his foot against the wall behind him.

"Go with the kids," I reprimand.

"No," he argues. "I'm the man in charge." I stare at my younger brother, wondering where this sudden urge came from.

"Charles, just because you're the oldest son doesn't

mean you have to be in charge. Let me get us what we need, and I'll bring it to the room." He crosses his arms over his chest. "I promise I'll be fine."

"Tell me where you're finding the food."

"Why does it matter? As long as we have food to eat, it doesn't matter where it comes from."

"Elsie, are you *doing* things with these men to get our food?"

"What? No!"

He looks around the main deck. "There doesn't seem to be a market anywhere nearby. I'm young, but I'm not naive. I know how things work."

I step toward my brother, placing a hand on his arm. "I appreciate your concern, but no, I'm not *doing* anything to get food. I have my ways."

His stance eases slightly. "Do you promise?"

"I promise." I squeeze his arm as I speak.

Charles's eyes grow several inches as Thorne approaches the two of us. "Good evening, Miss Abernathy."

I bow slightly. "Good evening, Captain. This is my brother, Charles." I watch the two men shake hands.

"Would you care to join me in my quarters tonight for a meal?" Thorne asks, looking between the two of us. "Both of you?"

"In the captain's quarters?" Charles asks.

"Aye, that would be where I eat. Better than that, please bring your entire family."

"Oh, no. We couldn't do that. Thank you for the

offer, but that would be asking too much. There are ten of us," I answer, pulling my brother toward the door to escape.

"I insist," Thorne continues.

"He insists, Elsie," Charles whispers. "We can't ignore what the captain insists upon."

"He's right," Thorne says behind me.

I close my eyes in defeat and turn, facing the giant man. "Thank you for the invitation. I will let my mother know." I smile, trying to hide the turmoil in my soul.

"I'll get them," Charles says as he disappears, leaving me alone with Thorne.

"Thank you for the invitation." I bow slightly with my words.

"Of course." My family exits the narrow door several seconds later, saving me from the awkwardness forming between us.

"Captain," Mama says with a deep bow. My sisters follow her movements, making me smile. "Thank you for the invitation."

"My pleasure, ma'am. I relish the company." He turns, moving toward the back of the ship. "Please, follow me."

I wait for everyone to pass before following them into the extravagant room at the back of the ship. I'm surprised at the difference between his quarters and ours. The room is as wide as the ship with a large table sitting in the middle. The room the men were playing cards in the other night is nothing compared to this one.

A lavishly decorated bed sits against the far wall. Beside it sits a desk covered in books and papers. A large window spans the entire length of the room, allowing a full view of the setting sun. "Is this a castle?" Bonnie asks, looking around the room with her small mouth gaping open.

"No, nothing that fancy. This is the captain's quarters," Thorne answers. "Please, sit down." He motions to the large table in the middle of the room. There are enough chairs for each person to have their own seat. Thorne pulls a chair out for Mama on one side of him, motioning for her to sit down. I can't help but notice her cheeks take on a pink hue as she does. He moves to the chair on his other side, pulling it out for me, before he sits between us. I try not to show the excitement I feel at sitting next to him.

"Thank you for taking me up on the offer. Dinner will be served shortly."

On cue, Smith enters the room, carrying a large platter of chicken. "I didn't realize you had company, Captain." His Scottish accent is one of the strongest I've heard.

"Just a few more mouths," he answers.

"Oh, that will be more than enough for all of us," Mama interrupts. "We don't eat much."

"Nonsense," he answers. "You all look like you

could use a good meal." He turns toward Smith. "Bring more chicken."

"Aye, Captain." Smith retreats from the quarters.

"Mama? May I have a piece?" Bonnie asks from my side.

"Of course you can, wee one." Thorne stands, taking the tray of food with him. He takes his time, filling each plate around the table until there is no more chicken on the platter.

"What about you?" Mama asks. "Are you not going to eat?"

He pats his stomach dramatically. "I ate earlier. I couldn't eat another bite."

His lies warm my heart. I take pleasure in watching the little ones tear into the first meal we've had in weeks. The smiles that cover their faces bring joy.

"How long have you been a captain?" Mama asks. "You look terribly young to be in charge of such a large vessel."

"Mama," I whisper.

"No, it's all right," Thorne answers. "As far as captains go, I *am* young. Mrs. Abernathy is correct. I am young to be in charge of a ship of this size." He stands, moving across the room. "The honor of becoming captain is partly because of my ability and partly because of my family name. The Rex family is very well-known in the shipping business. Once we arrive in America, I plan to expand our business to a new country."

"Do you think I could be a captain one day?" Bertram asks.

"If that's what you want," he answers. "Of course you can."

Smith walks back into the room, carrying another platter of chicken. I watch as Thorne places more food on the plates of my siblings who are still eating. "I can't thank you enough for this meal," Mama says, eating her second piece. "It's been a while since we've eaten a meal together as a family."

"In that case, I insist you all eat with me every evening."

"Oh, no, we couldn't..." Mama starts.

"Nonsense," Thorne interrupts. "I insist."

"Can we, Mama? Please?" Bonnie asks from the other side of the table.

"We'll see," she answers.

We spend the next hour listening to Thorne's stories of growing up on the sea. The more I'm around him, the more comfortable I feel, and the more attractive he becomes. I've never been around someone like him before, and my emotions betray me with thoughts of spending the rest of my life with him. *Don't be ridiculous, Elsie. As soon as you have a spell, he'll be like all the rest.* The voice in my head brings me back to reality.

"Thank you for the meal, Captain," Mama says, standing from the table. "It's getting late, and the children need their rest."

"Of course, Mrs. Abernathy. Thank you for the company. It's been a while since I've shared my table."

She stands, gathering my siblings. They head toward the door when Mama turns back toward me. "Elsbeth?"

"I'll be there in a minute."

She nods, giving me a smile of approval. I stare at the back of her head as she exits with my family in tow. Her smile brings the butterflies to life again. I've been around men all my life, but something about Thorne feels different.

"Thank you for dinner," I say after they've left his quarters.

"My pleasure, Elsbeth. My offer is sincere. Your family needs to eat and with no father in the picture—"

"My father is dead," I interrupt. "It wasn't his choice to not be in the picture."

Thorne stands straighter. "Of course. It wasn't my intention to infer anything otherwise." He clears his throat. "I apologize if my choice of words offended you."

I look down, not sure which crack in the floorboard to stare at. "No. It's me who should apologize. My father and I were very close. The thought of his reputation being damaged isn't something I'm prepared to think about."

"I understand." I look up, making eye contact. Gray eyes stare back at me, offering warmth through our connection. Thorne glances between my eyes and my mouth. "Thank you for dinner, Captain," I repeat, suddenly feeling out of sorts.

"You said that already," he reminds me.

"I did, didn't I?"

Large fingers wrap around mine as he pulls my hand to his lips, kissing the back. Tingles run down the length of my spine. I don't know whether to stand here, hoping for another hand kiss, or to turn and exit gracefully. Who am I kidding? I don't do anything gracefully.

Pulling my hand slowly from his, I turn toward the door. Just like the last two times we've spoken, I feel his eyes follow me through the door. Once outside, the breeze hits me, lifting several loose tendrils of hair with it.

I move closer to the rail, overlooking the glassy sea below, hoping to make sense of the plethora of emotions I feel running through my soul. "Elsbeth," a voice whispers from below, drawing me back to reality. I recognize it as the same voice as before.

"Where are you?" I shout over the edge. "Who are you?"

"Who *we* are will soon be discovered. Until then, my dear."

Am I losing my mind? Seconds later, a feeling that's been hidden for the past month boils its way to the surface. The sea below forms the familiar wiggles, telling me I must sit quickly. Before I'm able to obey my body, my legs and hands become numb, causing me to lose control of my extremities.

No! This can't be happening again. I collapse on the deck behind me, hitting my head with the fall. The stars above me begin their familiar dance as my body convulses completely. My legs coil to my chest, along with my arms. My body is no longer under my control.

"Elsbeth!" a deep voice calls from somewhere nearby. "Oh, my God. Elsbeth." Arms wrap around me, lifting my spasming body. "What's happening?" the voice asks. It feels familiar and strange at the same time.

My body is laid on top of something soft. The convulsions have slowed down, but are still out of my control. "Tell me what to do," the voice pleads. "I don't know how to help you."

The spasms continue to lessen, alerting me that it's almost over. The pain in my body releases, allowing me to slowly gain enough control to realize I'm back in Thorn's quarters. He's standing over me, his face covered in worry.

"I'm okay," my voice answers. The shakiness sounds through.

"Elsbeth, you were convulsing on the deck."

"I'm s...s...sorry."

"I'm not asking for an apology. What can I do to help?"

"Water," I whisper. "Thirsty."

He disappears from the bedside and moves quickly across the room, returning with a pint of something. "Drink." He pulls me forward, bringing the cup to my lips. The water fills the need my body desires. He lays me back on the softness of his bed and lays a cold cloth on my forehead.

"Thank you," I whisper. "Sleep." My eyes feel heavy, making it nearly impossible to keep them open. I know from experience that sleep is the only way I'm able to overcome this nightmare that has plagued me since childhood.

"Sleep," Thorne says. "I'll let your mother know you're okay." His voice trails off as I lose the battle, and the room fades to nothing.

……

My eyes open to an unfamiliar environment. Whenever these "fits" occur, my brain feels like mush for hours, sometimes days, later. I turn, finding the slumped-over body of Thorne in a chair that's two sizes too small.

Looking around, memories of him bringing me to his quarters surface, meaning he was the one who found me. "Hey," I whisper toward the sleeping giant.

Thorne's eyes open immediately. "Elsbeth? You're awake."

"I am." My voice sounds tired, even to me. I struggle, trying to sit up.

"Let me help you," he says, jumping to my side and sliding his arm behind me. He lifts me slightly, making it easier to lean against the large window above the bed. Once in place, he stares at me silently.

"You're curious," I fill in the blanks.

"I don't want to pry."

I close my eyes, not sure how to explain what I don't understand. "People in the village said I was possessed."

Thorne sits back in his chair. "That's dumb."

The simplicity of his words brings a smile to my face. "It's one of the reasons we're going to America."

"You will be able to find help?"

I nod. "I think so." I look down at my hands, full of small scratches from whatever I hit when I collapsed. "I hope so."

"I'm sorry, Elsbeth."

"Me, too," I answer. "They've caused nothing but pain for my family." I don't elaborate, and thankfully, he doesn't ask. I yawn with my words.

"Get some rest. I'll stay with you."

I don't question his words. Instead, my eyes close, welcoming me back into a world of silence.

bath, food, and pirates: not necessarily in that order

"ELSBETH." My mother's voice echoes through my mind. I fight to open my eyes, willing them to cooperate. "How is she?" she asks.

"She woke up yesterday and talked to me a little. Her color has returned," a deep voice answers. Yesterday? How long have I been asleep?

"Bless you, sir. You didn't have to stay with her the entire time. She could've come back to our room."

Heavy boots move across a wooden floor. "How long has she had these...these convulsions?"

"Since she was a baby," Mama answers.

"When she woke up, she told me the villagers thought she was possessed. Is that true?"

"Aye," Mama answers softly. "She was an outcast and forbidden to marry."

The sound of a deep sigh fills the room. "That's

preposterous. She's no more possessed than anyone else on the ship."

"Aye. After...after her father died, we had no choice but to leave our home."

"I'm sorry, Mrs. Abernathy."

"Aye, me too."

My eyes still refuse to open to join in the conversation that's all about me. "If you're okay with it, I'd like to keep her in here where I can watch her."

"What about your position?" Mama asks.

"Smith can handle it. Elsbeth is more important at the moment."

"Aye, she is. Thank you, Captain Rex." I hear the door close, taking what I assume is my mother out of the room.

Heavy boots move closer. "Continue to heal, acushla." I recognize the Gaelic term of endearment he uses for me. Why?

......

I have no idea how much time has passed when my eyes finally open again. Just as he promised, Thorne is still by my side, asleep in the chair. My father would sit with me after my fits. Seeing Thorne in the same position brings tears to my eyes and emotions I'm not prepared to deal with to the surface.

"Thorne?" I wake him.

"Elsbeth?"

"Aye. I'm better." I sit up, using my own strength. "How long have I been in your room?"

"Three days," he answers.

I stare at the giant man in front of me. A short beard has grown on his previously clean-shaven face. His hair is disheveled, and his clothes are a wrinkled mess. "Are you okay?"

A smile covers his face as he lifts one side of his mouth higher than the other. "Aye. Your mother has been by many times to check on you."

"She worries about me."

"She's not the only one."

I stretch my legs and slide them to the edge of his bed. "Thank you for taking care of me." I stand, wobbling on my weak limbs. Thorne is at my side instantly, helping steady me.

"How about some fresh air?"

"I'd love that." He wraps my arm through his, and we carefully move to a private deck off the back of the ship. The wind is just what I needed. I take a deep breath, filling my lungs with the sea air.

"Your mother told me you had to leave after your father died."

"Aye. Mama had no way to earn an income."

"I'm sorry about your father. I imagine that was hard."

"It was my fault." Thorne stares at me in silence. I close my eyes, willing the words to come out without tears. "I was working with him in the field near our home. It was something all the children did daily." I take a deep breath, clearing my mind. "That morning, my father and I were working on a new field he wanted to plant for the next season. My brothers were on the opposite field, planting seeds." I look over the railing, focusing on the sea below. "I began to convulse. I was tired and thirsty, which makes the spells worse. My father ran to help me. When he reached me, I was shaking so badly that he wasn't able to hold me. He fell backward, hitting his head on one of the rocks waiting to be cleared." I wipe tears from my eyes. "He died, and I couldn't do anything but watch him bleed to death as I shook uncontrollably. It was my fault. I killed him."

"Elsbeth, I'm so sorry. You have to know it wasn't your fault. You had nothing to do with his falling. It was a horrible accident."

"It was my fault. If he hadn't tried to help me, he wouldn't have fallen. I killed him."

Thorne wraps his arm around my shoulders, pulling me to his side. "I'm so sorry." I don't answer. Instead, I bury my head into his shoulder. The warmth of his touch is almost more than I can handle. I've never been this close to a man, for that matter, never wanted to. Being this close to Thorne, I want more. Several minutes of silence pass before he pulls away, allowing the cold air to seep where we were once connected. "You need to eat."

My stomach growls on command. "I usually can't hold anything down for a while when this happens."

"How about soup? I can ask the cook to make some fresh soup."

"I could use a bath. I feel gross."

Thorne smiles. "I can make that happen." He turns, pulling me gently behind his back into his quarters. He moves quickly to a long box against the wall, lifting the top off. I see the glimmer of a metal tub inside. "I'll have one of the women come to help you."

"Seriously? I can use your bathtub?"

"Aye." He smiles wide with my excitement. He guides me to the tub, pulling it from the cabinet. "If you'll excuse me, I'll go find the young woman for the water and see about that soup."

"Thank you." My words feel inadequate.

"You're welcome, Elsbeth." His eyes linger on mine for longer than necessary. "Excuse me," he whispers before leaving me alone in the lavish room. I don't know how to wait and feel awkward trying to figure it out. Thankfully, I don't wait long before the young girl I recognize from fleeing our stateroom enters the quarters.

"Hello," she says with a wide smile.

"Hello," I answer.

"Captain Rex asked me to bring you hot water for a bath."

"Thank you," I answer, still not sure what to say.

"My name is Cora. What's yours?"

"Elsbeth. How old are you?"

"Seventeen."

"Are you alone on the ship?"

Cora laughs. "No, my father works for Captain Rex. I'm allowed to come with him."

"You like being here?"

She shrugs. "I guess. Can I help you undress?"

"No." I shake my head for extra emphasis. "I can manage. Can I help you with the water?"

"I'm going to heat it over the fire. It shouldn't take long."

She pulls a heavy pot from a spot I hadn't even noticed and hangs it on a hook in the fireplace. I watch as she moves toward the tub, pulling a dressing screen from the wall and spreading it in front of the tub area. "This will give you some privacy." She pulls a few items from the cabinet, setting them next to the tub. "Here is some lye."

"Thank you, Cora." I slip behind the screen and slowly pull my gross clothes away from my body. I smell like a sailor who's been at sea for a year. Lowering into the tub, I wrap my arms around me, feeling exposed.

"Coming in," she warns, bringing the hot cauldron with her. "It doesn't take long in this pot. Pull your feet back so ya don't get burned."

I do as she suggests, and she pours the water into the tub. The moment the heat hits me, my muscles relax almost instantly. The water stops at my waist. "I'm going to get a bit more," she says, disappearing from behind the screen. I lie back in the tub, relishing the heat as it passes through my body.

Cora returns quickly, pouring more water and bringing the level to my neck. "Thank you."

"Aye, you keep saying that." She laughs as she speaks.

"It's because I'm grateful." I laugh with her.

"I'll give you some privacy. Captain Rex requested soup for ya. I'll bring it back after you're clean."

"Than—"

"Don't thank me, Elsbeth. It's my job." She disappears, leaving me alone in the room. Sinking into the tub, I lower my head under the water. It takes three scrubs with the soap before I begin to feel like my hair is clean. I scrub the rest of my body, not surprised that the water turns cloudy almost instantly.

"I brought you some soup and a clean dress," Cora announces, coming back into the room.

"A clean dress?" I've worn the same dress for the past month.

"Aye. It's got a few mended holes, but it's clean and smells better than the one you're wearing." She sets the clean clothes behind the screen. "You'll find a cloth to dry yourself with there as well."

I climb from the now cold water and find the clothes and drying cloth she left for me. The fabric of the cloth is rough but feels good against my skin. The dress is worn but she's right. It smells good and is soft. I put on the different layers, relishing the cleanliness.

Several minutes later, I slide back the screen, finding a steaming bowl of soup waiting on the table.

"It's not much," Cora says, picking up the rags of my original dress. "I hope you like mushrooms."

"It smells wonderful," I answer, taking the spoon into my mouth. After a hot bath and a warm meal, I feel better than I have in a while.

"I'll leave you to it," Cora says, leaving me alone again.

I finish the soup, making sure to clean up the mess from my bath. "You look beautiful," Thorne says, coming back into the room.

"Thank you. I smell better." I laugh.

"Shall we go for a walk on deck, Miss Abernathy?" His thick Scottish brogue turns into formal English as he offers me his arm.

"Aye, I'd like that."

He loops my arm through his, and we exit the main door, heading toward the helm. "Captain on deck!" Smith yells from behind the wheel. I watch as the men stop what they're doing and salute Thorne.

"Do they always do that?" I ask.

"Aye. It feels a little too formal to me, but it's required, so I deal with it."

"Captain?" Smith says from the helm. "The lookouts have spotted a ship in the distance."

"What kind of ship?" he asks.

"Too far away to know. She's got four sails." The two men share a look.

"What does that mean?" I ask.

Thorne turns back toward me. "It's too early to know. Most likely a cargo vessel on its way back home." He turns back to his first mate. "Keep me informed."

"Aye, Captain." We walk toward the bow of the ship, allowing Thorne to get a better view of the approaching vessel.

"Should we be worried?"

"We'll soon find out. They're clearly moving in our direction."

"Are you concerned?"

"Nothing to be concerned about at this point." The tone of his voice betrays his words.

I stare into the sea, trying to get a better view. Other than the sails, I can't see much. Movement below grabs my attention. "What was that?" I ask, pointing at the water.

"I don't see anything. What did you see?"

"I'm not sure. Something large breached the surface."

Thorne peers over the deck. "Most likely a dolphin. My men caught an injured one a few weeks ago. Sometimes they like to swim with the ships."

I stare into the water, seeing the movement again. This time something that looks like dark fabric surfaces before disappearing again. "Do dolphins wear clothes?"

"What?" he asks, following my line of sight. "What did you see?"

"I'm not sure, but it looked like fabric." Together,

we look over the side. When the creature surfaces again, it's obvious that it's not a dolphin. "What was that, Thorne?"

"I don't know," he answers. He turns toward the helm. "Smith, do you see anything in the water?"

"No, sir!" he yells back. "Spotters!" Smith yells toward the men on top of the lookout post. "Is there something in the water?"

The men above stare down, searching for what we just saw. When the creature breaches the surface for the third time, it's obvious there is no creature, but a man. "What the hell?" Thorne whispers. "Elsbeth, get inside."

"She stays," the voice I heard from the water days earlier whispers. A man emerges from the water, fully dressed. He climbs the bow of the ship, scaling the wood unlike any human I've ever seen.

"Elsbeth, get to safety, please." Thorne pulls a long sword from his belt, holding it between me and the creature.

I turn, ready to follow orders, when the man jumps onto the deck several feet in front of us. "Maybe you misunderstood me," he hisses. "I said, she stays." He's wearing black pants and a loose-fitting black shirt. His dark hair is tied behind his neck and tied with a black cloth.

"Who are you, sir?" Thorne asks.

The man moves closer. His movements remind me of a predator on the prowl.

"Who I am is of no concern. Give me the girl."

"You are in no position to demand anything of me, sir," Thorne retorts. "You are trespassing on my ship, and I demand you leave."

The man laughs, showing two sharp teeth in front. Chill bumps cover my skin. "I don't believe you are in the position to demand anything." He looks around the ship, spotting the sailors awaiting their leader's command. "Your men will be no help to you."

"Those men will kill you on my word."

The creature moves so fast, I can't track him. A scream sounds from my right. I turn, finding a young sailor lying in a pool of blood and the creature behind him. "How efficient are your men now?"

"What the bloody hell?" Thorne asks.

"Should I kill a few more?" the man responds. "Give me Elsbeth." His words are slow and calculated.

"What do you want with me?" I ask. My voice is no louder than a whisper.

He stalks closer. "Your pain calls to me. I can help you. I can fix the convulsions and make you live forever. Free of your pain. Free of the demonic possession that fills you."

"I am not possessed."

The creature laughs. "You don't truly believe that. You didn't believe that after you killed your father."

"How...how do you know about that?"

He smiles, showing the sharp teeth again. "I have my ways."

"I don't want to live forever."

"Surrender yourself, or everyone aboard this vessel will die."

Thorne moves closer to the man. "You'll have to go through me first."

"I like that idea," he responds.

"No. I won't allow you to die for me." I turn back toward the creature. "If I go with you, do I have your word that you will spare the rest of the ship?"

"Yes," his voice slurs.

"Elsbeth, you can't possibly be considering this. He's not a threat. My men will take him."

"Your naivety is amusing." He turns toward the oncoming ship. "That ship contains many of my kind. You won't win. We will slaughter every soul on board, starting with you and her family." He licks his lips, turning toward me. "They're below, aren't they?" He lifts his head to the sky. "I can smell them from here."

Thorne raises his sword high, charging at the creature. The man moves seconds before Thorne makes contact with him, sending the captain into the railing. He turns quickly, finding the creature on the other side of him. "How do you move so quickly?"

A deep laugh echoes off the sea below. "It's simply what I do, boy." He turns back toward me. "Come now, Elsbeth. Is his death worth it? Are *their* deaths worth it?" He motions to the crowd gathered around, swords held at their chest.

"Elsbeth?" a familiar voice says from behind me. I

turn, finding Charles standing in the doorway to the stateroom hall. "What's going on?"

"Go back to the room now!" I demand.

The creature lifts his nose high in the air once more and smiles. "Your brother is calling you, Elsbeth. He *is* your brother, isn't he? I smell the family bond."

"Elsie?" Charles continues.

"Charles, go inside."

"Yes, Charles, go inside," the creature mimics my words.

"Captain, the ship is close!" a man yells from the lookout.

"Oh, look. They're here." He turns back toward me. "Come, Elsbeth."

Thorne raises his sword high. "She's not going anywhere with you."

"Are you going to let him make decisions for you? I thought you were stronger than that."

"I'm not going with you."

I blink, and the creature is gone. Fear fills me. I turn, finding my worst fear coming true. Charles's eyes are huge as the monster stands behind him with long fingernails pressed against his throat.

"No!" I scream. "Leave him alone."

Charles closes his eyes, hoping to hide the tear that just escaped. "Take me instead," he whispers.

"How sweet. The relationship between siblings isn't always so loving."

The creature's mouth contorts, and the fangs from

earlier grow even larger. He bites into Charles's neck. Seconds later, his lifeless body lands with a sickening thud on the deck.

"Vampire," Smith whispers from the helm.

The creature turns toward the first mate and bows dramatically. "One of the many names my kind are called."

"Charles," I cry toward the lifeless body of my brother. Blood surrounds his remains. Memories of my father's body, lying in a similar pool of blood, flood into my mind.

"Come, Elsbeth," the creature says, reaching his hand toward me.

"No!" Thorne warns. "I won't allow it."

"Clearly, you are in no position to *allow* anything." He turns toward me. "Once that ship reaches this one, everyone will die. Come with me now, and I'll allow them to live."

"Everyone?" My voice is shaky.

"Everyone," he echoes.

I slip my hand inside of his and close my eyes. "Good girl," he says before lifting me into the sky.

"Elsbeth!" Thorne's voice is the last thing I hear before the world goes dark.

captive

THE SMELL of copper and death fills my nose as I fight to open my eyes. I recognize the smell immediately as blood. My mind replays the events of Charles's death and being taken by the creature. That was a dream. It had to be a dream. There's no other explanation. The sensation of something wet sliding down my cheek lets me know I am awake.

I'm lying on something hard, and my body is in a strange position, with my legs curled underneath. The more aware I become, the more I realize everything hurts.

"Hello?" I try to call out.

"Shut up, girl. Are you dumb?" a hoarse voice says from somewhere in the room.

"Where am I?"

The voice laughs, sounding more animalistic than human. "You're aboard Kragen's ship."

"Kragen?"

"Aye, the vampire that brought you here."

"Vampire?" I ask, remembering the same word Smith said before the creature lifted me into the sky. "They're real?"

The voice laughs again. "Very much so."

"Who are you?" I struggle to sit up, not able to move much of anything.

"I am no one. At least not anymore." The voice sounds sad. "I used to be someone once upon a time. Now I'm just a shell of a human as you will be soon."

I slide my back against something solid and lower my head into my hands. "I can't see anything."

"That's because we're in the bottom of the ship. There are no windows or light. Your eyes will adjust."

"Are we alone?"

"We are not alone, but we're the only ones living."

Sliding my hand around, I bump into something cold and solid. Oh, my God. I remember that feeling from my father. There's a dead body next to me. I can't control the tears that flow.

"Don't waste your water," the voice warns. "You'll need everything you can get. Most of them die from dehydration or starvation. You choose."

"How long have you been here?"

"I don't know. A few days, weeks, months." The voice gets quiet. "I've lost track at this point. I must not be very tasty. I'm still alive."

"Tasty?"

"Why do you think you're here, girl?" I don't answer. "You're here as a snack when they can't go on land."

"A snack?"

"Have you lived your whole life in a hole? They're vampires. You're on a ship full of pirate vampires. They have to eat, and we're their food."

I stare toward the voice for what seems like an eternity before being able to process his words. "We're their food?" I repeat.

"More like a blood donor...an unwilling blood donor."

On cue, a door opens, flooding the dark room with dim light. "Get the boy," a man says. My eyes won't focus on who or what's coming through the door.

Instinctively, I close my eyes, pretending to be passed out or dead. Whichever works the best.

"I'm empty," the weary voice says from across the room. "There's nothing left."

"I can smell ya, mate. You're good for at least a few more feedin's," a man answers. The sound of grunting and something being drug over a wooden surface pierces my ears.

"It's time to dump some of these bodies," a different voice says. "They're starting to smell."

"Nah, leave 'em. They're food for the rats."

"I ain't eatin' no rats." The two men share a laugh, making me sick to my stomach. "What about that one?"

"Cap'n says hands off. That one is his." I know without asking, they're talking about me.

"I can smell her blood from here."

"Aye, me, too." The door closes, taking the light with it.

I can't stop the tears from flowing. I try to stand without much luck. My legs are weak and barely able to hold my weight. Seconds later, I fall to the ground, landing on something solid and cold. Another body. My stomach empties onto the floor in front of me. This is how I'm going to die. Being held captive by a band of vampire pirates.

My mind flashes back to Charles and his lifeless body collapsed on the deck of Thorne's ship. My poor mother. Losing her husband, son, and daughter so close together. I've never felt so helpless.

The door opens not long after and provides enough light to see the room is littered with corpses. I can't make out any details, other than they're lifeless. Another body is thrown back into the room, landing with a crunch.

I wait until the door closes again before speaking. "Are you all right?" I whisper, receiving no response. "Hello?"

I know without being able to see that the person who was talking to me earlier is now dead, joining the rest of the corpses on the floor. I'm alone. I'm truly alone.

I have no idea how much time has passed, and no

one has been back in the room since returning my only companion. My stomach rumbles louder than I thought possible, echoing through the small room. My lips and mouth are caked in sores from thirst. I don't need a doctor to tell me I won't make it much longer. I'm dying. Maybe that's what he wants?

Out of nowhere, a feeling I recognize hits me hard. My legs and arms begin to cramp, curling me into a small ball in the area I've claimed as my own. Without food or water, my body is out of my control. When the convulsions begin, my body is thrown around stronger than ever before. The sound leaving my throat is terrifying, even to me. It's a mixture of a cry, a scream, and death all rolled into one. I'm going to die alone, surrounded by bodies, in the bottom of a pirate ship.

Dim light floods the room, and my body is lifted off the floor. Seconds later, light floods my eyes, and the heat of the sun covers me.

"Tsk, tsk, tsk," a familiar voice clicks. "It seems your demon has come out to play."

"I'm not possessed," my mind screams.

"I can take this pain from you, but what shall I do for a food source until the next port?" He leans against the wall, watching me, relishing the pain wracking my body.

I know what he's offering. He's going to make me one of them. One of the bloodsuckers. One of the killers. *"I'd rather die!"* my mind screams.

"Careful there. You don't want to bruise that beautiful skin of yours." His laugh fills my ringing ears. "Oh, all right. You've talked me into it. Your heartbeat is slowing down, which means you're about to die, my dear. I simply cannot allow that to happen."

"Let me die..."

He lifts me into his arms, forcibly holding my body still. I don't see what pierces my neck, but my body reacts instantly. The sun begins to fade, leaving only a small circle of light. I'm dying...I'm dead.

......

The smell of death surrounds me. From the feel of the floor beneath me and the bodies around me, I'm still in the bottom of the ship, surrounded by death. Every part of my body aches. The blood filling my body is on fire. My heart is pounding out of my chest. I want to die.

"Is she still alive?" a voice I don't recognize asks.

"Aye, looks that way," a second voice laughs deeply. "Smells that way, too."

"I knew I shoulda drained her when I had the chance," the first voice answers.

"That's a good way to die, that is."

"Grab that one over there." I feel something next to me move followed by a faint cry.

"No, please," a young woman begs. "Let me go, and I won't tell anyone about you."

The two lower voices share a laugh. "Did ya hear that? She won't tell anyone about us?"

Her soft whimpers become screams as she kicks into my leg. *"Help me!"* I scream through my mind.

A loud thud echoes through the room, and the cries stop. "Dammit, you killed her. You know I don't like to eat from something dead. It tastes weird."

"Her blood's still warm. There's enough for both of us." The sound of sucking makes my stomach turn. Several minutes pass before the weight of a body is thrown on top of me and the door creaks closed.

What kind of hell am I in?

......

My eyes open to darkness, but unlike before, the room isn't black. Sitting up is easier and gives me the ability to see that I'm surrounded by dozens of decaying bodies. "Is anyone alive?" I whisper. No one responds.

My stomach growls loud enough to echo through the room, causing me to double over in pain. I've never been so hungry. Going weeks without eating never made me this hungry before.

Something scurries past my foot. Without thinking, I grab it, realizing it's a rat the size of a small dog. I bite into its body, draining it of every ounce of blood inside. Throwing the empty vessel to the floor, I'm appalled by what I did but craving more.

Did I just drain the blood from a rat? My stomach growls, begging for more. I've lost count of how many rats I've drained, as I sit, surrounded by corpses. My mind hasn't caught up with my body, and I begin to try to make sense of what's happened.

I stand, wading through the sea of bodies, and move toward the door. "Hello!" I scream, not caring who hears me. "Help me!" My voice sounds guttural and inhuman. "I'm hungry!"

Time slows down as I sit alone, waiting for someone to open the door. No one comes. Even the rats hide from me.

......

"Good evening, my dear," Kragen says, entering the room that's now my own. My legs and arms are bound behind me, wrapped in chains made from silver. The metal burns into my skin, leaving me bloody from the constant injuries.

"Shut up," I spew.

He laughs. "Seems we're in a good mood today."

In his hands is a glass of fresh blood. The smell makes me rabid with desire. My breathing picks up as the scent fills my body.

"Is this what you want?" He taunts me, holding the glass closer before taking several sips. He makes a face. "Tastes a bit...stale." He throws the glass and its contents against the far wall, smashing the glass along with the blood my body calls for.

"Oops," he says with a laugh. "Did you want that?" He stands, leaving my side. "You smell like shit. It's time for a bath."

I resist the urge to close my eyes at the thought of what Kragen's baths entail. He moves toward the door. "Elliot," he says softly. Seconds later, a young man with white blonde hair opens the door.

"Yes, sir?"

"She smells. It's time for a bath."

"Sir?" the young boy questions. "The last time nearly killed her."

Kragen stares at the boy. "Are you questioning me? She's a vampire. She can't die."

"No, sir." The boy bows his head in submission. "How long, sir?"

Kragen turns back toward me. "A week should be sufficient."

A week? I refuse to react to his words. Although he holds every ounce of power over me, I refuse to let him know it.

"Yes, sir," Elliot answers. Kragen leaves the room, and Elliot moves to my side.

"Elsbeth, I'm sorry," he whispers. "I don't have a choice."

I refuse to make eye contact with him.

Elliot looks around the room before pulling something from his pocket. "Here, I brought this for you." He hands me a small satchel full of blood. "It's fresh."

I don't wait to be told again. I empty the contents in one gulp, feeling the sensation flow through my body, quenching the thirst my body demands. "Thank you, Elliot."

"You're welcome. I'm sorry for what I have to do." I nod, understanding he has no choice. "Play nice," he begs as he pulls me to my feet.

"Take off the chains, and I will."

"You know I can't do that." He tugs, pulling me forward. With the addition of silver, my body is weak and unable to fight against the younger vampire.

"What year is it?" I ask as we work our way toward the deck.

"1808," Elliot answers.

I stop walking, realizing I've been on this ship for nearly one hundred years. "You have to help me, Elliot. I don't belong here."

He closes his eyes. "I know, and I'm sorry. The blood is the only thing I can do right now." He leads me to the back of the ship, wrapping the now familiar anchor chain around my waist. "I'm sorry, Elsbeth. Just relax, and it will be over soon."

I fight to keep the tears from flowing and nod at his words. He's right. There's no point in fighting. I'm not strong enough to fight Kragen. My only hope is to escape.

Elliot turns me toward the water and knocks me into the stream that follows the ship. Even though a vampire doesn't need to breathe, the sensation of drowning is terrifying as my body bobs up and down under the water for the next week.

the cost of freedom

"ELSBETH, I brought you something to eat," Elliot whispers, coming into the room. "It's not fresh, but it's better than nothing."

I take the small bag of blood, and the smell turns my stomach. "How old is it?"

He shrugs. "A week or so. I'm sorry. It was all I could find."

"It's fine." I drink the contents, focusing on not allowing myself to smell the foul odor. I resist the urge to gag. "Thank you, Elliot."

"We are docking off the coast of New York in a few weeks, and Kragen is taking most of the men onto shore."

"Why are you telling me this?"

He shifts from one foot to the other. "Because it might be your chance to escape."

I lift the chains high. "Even if I have the chance, these chains weaken me and will keep me in place."

"Not if I can get the key," he interrupts.

"Kragen keeps the key tied around his neck. There's no way you can do that without getting yourself killed."

"If I can get the key, we can be together."

Elliot is young, naive, and thankfully in love with me. He's the only reason I'm still alive. I owe him my life. "I'd like that," I lie. While Elliot has kept me alive physically, thoughts of Thorne have kept me alive mentally.

Daydreams of Thorne walking down the aisle with a beautiful woman on his arm, bouncing overactive children on his knee, and thoughts of my family thriving in America are what's kept me going all this time. I did this so they could live: my family, the crew, and everyone on his ship.

The blood Elliot brought me churns in my stomach, making me nauseous.

"I'm going to get you out of here," Elliot interrupts my thoughts.

"Thank you, but don't make promises you can't keep."'

He covers my hand with his. "I'm not." He turns, leaving me chained in the dungeon that has been my home. I don't want to think about Elliot's words. Getting my hopes up will only result in pain.

The blood in my stomach churns once more,

making me throw up. I'd rather be dead. Why didn't Kragen just kill me?

......

The sound of keys rattling and the smell of sulfur draws my attention to the door. It's the unmistakable warning that Kragen is coming. I prepare myself for whatever might happen. "Oh, you're home," he says with a laugh as he enters. "I thought you might be out at the moment."

Asshole.

"I just got back," I retort. Instead of the scared little victim Kragen kidnapped, I've become the vampire bitch being held captive over the years.

Kragen's laugh fills the room. "That's why I keep you around. No one else would dare speak to me that way."

"I have nothing to lose."

"Aye, you don't. That's what makes you so fun."

"Fuck you, Kragen."

He pulls a pocket watch to his face. "Looks like we don't have time today. Plus, it's time for your bath. I need to remind Elliot of his duties. Oh, wait. I forgot. Elliot is dead."

I look up at his words. "What happened to him?"

He shrugs. "Somehow, his head fell off."

Kragen's words strike me in the gut. "You bastard," I whisper.

"First, you offer your body. Now you call me a bastard. You are quite finicky today." I don't respond, and he moves closer. "You're weak-minded, Elsie. That boy was feeding you. Do you think I don't know what happens on my ship?"

I stare down my captor, refusing to retreat. "Get out."

"Look at you, being all brave." He pulls the key to my chains from under his collar, setting it on the wooden floor just out of my reach. "Let's see how brave you actually are."

I fight the tears forming in my eyes. "Kill me," I whisper.

Kragen laughs again. "What would be the fun in that?" He leaves the room, closing the door behind him.

I stand, walking as far as the chains will allow, pulling against my restraints as hard as possible. It's something I've done millions of times over the years, and even though the pain of the silver burns my skin, the desire to be free is stronger. I stretch closer and closer to the key that's just beyond reach.

"No!" I scream as my fingers are mere inches away from the freedom they represent.

"Elsie," Elliot's voice says through the door. "Are you okay?"

"Elliot? You're alive?"

"Aye." He laughs softly. "Why wouldn't I be?"

"I need your help." The door creaks open, and Elliot is standing in the doorway...head attached.

"Is that...is that Kragen's key?"

"Aye. Is he on the ship?"

"No, they just left." He rushes to the key and then to the locks holding them in place.

"Unlock them," I demand.

Elliot follows orders. The pop of the lock is the most beautiful sound I've ever heard. He moves to my side, unlocking the locks around my wrists and ankles. The sound of the chains falling to the floor is almost more than I can handle.

"Thank you," I whisper, wrapping my arms around his thin neck.

"We need to go now," Elliot says, pulling back.

"How many are on board?"

"Three including me."

"We're going to have to kill them," I tell him.

"I know," he answers. For the first time in a century, I walk through the door of my room without chains attached.

"Elliot, this has to be a trick. Kragen told me you were dead. He doesn't make mistakes. This is too good to be true."

"Why would he do that?" He laces his fingers through mine, pulling me up the stairs toward the main deck. "Kragen's an ass, but even he's not that bad."

I reluctantly follow him to the empty deck. Fog covers the sea around us, and in the distance, the shadows of buildings peek through the open spaces. "Is that New York?" I ask.

"Aye. We'll have to swim to the coast." We move to the rail overlooking the sea below. "I'll jump first. You can follow me."

"What are ya doin', Elliot?" a man asks from behind us.

Elliot turns toward the voice. "We're goin' for a swim, Felix. Kragen left orders that she be cleaned. Since the ship isn't moving, I'm going in with her to make sure she doesn't escape."

A second man joins the first. "Is that what yer doin'? Takin' her for a swim?"

"Aye." The two men share a look.

"Elliot..." I warn.

"I know," he answers.

I turn, facing the two men. Both smile widely. I recognize them both from their "visits" to my room through the years. "Don't make me kill you," I warn.

Both men share a laugh. "Kill us? I think you're confused, little girl."

"I'm not confused. I have a hundred years of anger built up inside. I won't hesitate to use it. Let me go."

"We can't do that, wee one. Why don't you come over here, and we'll show you what you're good for?"

Rage fills me. Not a normal rage, but the kind of rage that's been building for a century. I don't bother with walking. Instead, I leap from the railing, directly in front of them. Wrapping my arms around each of their necks in unison, I twist both hands, ripping their heads from their bodies.

"Elsie," Elliot says from the railing. "You killed them."

"Aye, I warned you."

"How? You...you shouldn't be that strong."

"Elliot, I have to go, and you can't go with me."

I instantly regret my words. Out of everyone on this ship, Elliot was the only one who helped me. The only one who was nice to me. He kept me alive when Kragen tortured me.

"I love you, Elsie," he whispers.

"I can't let you come with me," I repeat. "I have to go alone. Kragen will never let me go. He will follow me no matter where I go, and you'll only slow me down." My words are cruel.

"Elsie," he begs.

"No, Elliot. You can't stay here, but you can't come with me."

He closes his eyes, sadness covering his face. "Okay," he whispers.

Out of nowhere, something runs between the two of us, knocking Elliot to the ground. I catch a glimpse of a girl, not much older than me, as she retreats behind a pole.

"Who are you?" I shout at her shadow.

She copies her movement from before, crossing between us, grabbing Elliot this time. Her dark auburn-colored hair is a tangle of mats, and her clothes are worn with holes. "I'll kill him," she warns.

"Who are you?" I repeat.

"I am death," she answers.

"Are you being held here against your will?"

She laughs. "I am death," she repeats, clearly out of her mind.

"Aubrey?" Elliot says, drawing the girl's attention to him.

"You're leaving with her?" she asks. "You said you loved me."

"I do, Aubrey." He closes his eyes.

I don't know what's going on, and Aubrey doesn't give me the time to figure it out. She pulls a wooden stake from her dress and moves in front of Elliot at vampire speed. She raises the stake, stabbing it through Elliot's heart with a guttural scream. I don't know who she is or how long she's been here, but she's insane.

"Aubrey," I start.

"Shut up, bitch," she yells, interrupting my words. She releases her hold on Elliot's body, which falls to the deck with a heavy thud.

"I'm leaving this ship. You can come with me if you like, but I'm not staying one minute longer."

"You can't leave," she mutters. "No one can leave. We're all captive here. We're all food here. We're all vampires here."

"Aubrey," I pull her attention back toward me. "I'm going to jump. If you try to stop me, I will defend myself. Do you understand what that means?"

"No one can leave," she begins repeating. "We're all food here. We're all vampires here."

I move to the top of the railing and prepare to jump when she wraps her arms around my thighs, pulling me back to the deck. "No one can leave. We're all captives here..."

"Aubrey!" I scream, slapping her across her cheek. "Wake the hell up."

I recognize the look in her eyes the moment she makes eye contact. She's going to kill me. Two sharp teeth protrude from her mouth, and she hisses, reminding me of a lion on the prowl. "No one can leave," she screams and jumps toward me.

I catch her in midair, throwing her body to the ground. She's back on her feet in an instant and moving quickly toward me.

"I will kill you this time," I warn.

She continues her assault, and I make good on my promise. Waiting until she's in the perfect position, I grab her neck, turn her back toward me, and pull her close. I bite into her neck, ripping her head from her body.

"I'm sorry, Aubrey. You deserved better." I turn toward what's left of Elliot. "Thank you, my friend."

I move back to the top of the railing, this time jumping into the water below.

monster

Boston, Massachusetts
1892

"EXCUSE ME, MISS?" a short older man says, interrupting my morning routine. In the two weeks I've been in Boston, coming to Franklin Park every morning with a book and a forlorn look has proven to be some of the best hunting of my life. The men in Boston are more than willing to try and take advantage of a young, lonely young woman.

"Yes?" I smile with my answer. "May I help you?"

"I wondered if I might join you?" he says, pointing at the empty spot next to me on the bench.

"I'd like that, thank you." I look behind him, searching for a family member who might be accompanying him.

"What brings you out here, alone?" he asks, sliding closer to my side.

"What makes you think I'm alone?" I flirt.

He looks around, mimicking my moves from earlier. "I don't see anyone but us out here."

I laugh. "I guess you're right." I close the novel I'm holding. "I enjoy coming out here. Time to myself is the best medicine."

"No truer words have ever been spoken." He looks around nervously before sliding closer. The sweat covering his brow makes my stomach growl with hunger. He slides his hand to my knee and squeezes.

"What are you doing, sir?" I ask, hoping to give him one last chance at redemption.

"It's what you're here for, isn't it?"

"I don't know what you're talking about. Please don't touch me." I'm proud of the nervousness that shines through my words. "I am a lady." I almost laugh out loud at the last part.

"A lady doesn't come to a park without a chaperone. How much?" he asks, sliding his hand up my arm, pushing the dress ruffles upward.

"I don't know what you're referring to, sir."

The man pulls his hand away and grabs his crotch, holding on tightly. "How much, whore?"

"I'm no whore, sir."

He raises his hand, slapping me across the face with the backside. "Suck it." He pulls open the buttons holding his pants in place, and exposes his erect penis.

Grabbing my perfectly styled hair, he pulls me toward his groin.

It's not the penis that excites me, but what lies next to it. The blood coursing through the artery in his thigh calls to me—begs for me to drink from it. He forces me to the ground in front of him and pushes my head further into him.

"Are you sure about this?" I ask, dropping all pretense of the scared single woman.

"Suck it, whore."

I don't try to disguise the fangs as they protrude from my mouth. Bypassing his penis, I move straight to the artery and latch on. Mere seconds pass before the man is drained of the blood that once flowed through his body.

I stand, wiping any remnants from my mouth, and look at the remains of my latest victim. His lifeless body is pale and empty-looking. Instead of giving him the dignity of pulling up his pants, I leave him exposed to anyone who might stumble upon his corpse. He doesn't deserve dignity.

London, England
1943

The number of bodies covering the street after the bombing is nearly overwhelming, even for me. The Germans have bombed the city for the past few days, destroying many city blocks. The few people who have ventured onto the streets are covered in dirt, and their clothes are full of holes.

"Where are you going, missy?" a voice says from an alleyway as I pass.

Seeing the number of humans that have died has taken my appetite away. I ignore the man and keep moving down what's left of the street.

"Did you hear me, bitch?" he repeats.

"Leave me alone," I warn and keep walking. The sound of a young child crying stops me in my tracks. I turn toward the sound, seeing the man whose voice I heard, holding a small girl in his arms. She can't be any older than six or seven, and from the looks of her clothes and hair, she's alone.

"My daughter needs a mother."

Something inside me clicks, telling me this girl isn't his daughter. I move in front of the man and the girl. "Are you all right, dear one?"

Tear stains cover her cheeks as the man squeezes her tightly. "She's fine, aren't you?" The girl nods. "See, she's just a little scared."

"Are you hungry?" I ask the child. She nods again.

"We're both hungry if you know what I mean," the man answers, looking me up and down.

"I'm hungry, too," I admit. However, my need to free this child has overcome my need to eat.

"I have some food up there." He points at a set of stairs that have been broken in several places from the bombing. "Why don't you come up, and I'll fix food for all of us?"

The girl looks at me with large eyes, begging for my help. The smell of copper fills my nose, and I realize she has blood covering her extremities. I know in an instant what he's done.

"Give her to me," I demand.

"Come on up and—" I don't wait for him to finish. I grab the girl and knock him to the wall behind him in one quick move. Moving with vampire speed, I take her around the corner, hiding her from what I'm about to do.

"Stay here, and I'll be right back." She nods at my words as fresh tears cover her face.

Seconds later, I'm in front of the man, pinning him against the wall. I don't waste time with formalities. "What did you do to her?"

"Nothing she didn't want." He smiles. "She needed someone to take care of her, and so did I."

"You're going to die now." I make sure he can see everything that's about to happen to him as I bring out the monster locked inside.

The scream that leaves his mouth is cut short as I sink my teeth into his neck, draining every ounce of blood inside his body. What's left of him slides into the rubble below. "Have fun in hell, asshole."

Back in front of the young girl, I hug her close, offering the loving comfort she's been denied, and take her to a hospital not far away.

"Can I help you, ma'am?" a woman wearing a white uniform asks as we enter the emergency room.

"I found her on the street. She was alone, and I think she's hurt."

"Thank you," the girl whispers as the woman takes her from my arms and ushers her toward a back room.

"Ma'am, I need your contact information," another woman says from a desk not far away.

I turn, leaving the hospital and the girl behind.

Los Angeles, California
1986

The number of humans covering the beach is almost overwhelming. Families with children in tow are hauling everything they own to the sand to spend a few hours on the water. I've lost track of the last time I ate, and my stomach growls at the memory.

"Shut the hell up, Frankie," a middle-aged woman warns as she drags a young boy across a scalding hot parking lot. He's not wearing shoes, and no doubt his bare feet are no match for the hot asphalt.

"Mama, it burns," the boy cries as she drags him.

She slaps him across the face. "I said shut up, boy. You'll be fine."

She's wearing a pair of blue jean shorts that are cut so short, they leave nothing to the imagination. The bikini top she's wearing is at least two sizes too small, and the cigarette hanging from her lips has nothing left to smoke.

"His feet are burning," I say to her, interrupting her trek.

"Mind your own business, bitch," she warns. "He's *my* son."

"*Your* son's feet are burning," I repeat. "He needs shoes." I slide my cheap jelly sandals off and hand them to the boy.

"My son isn't wearing girl shoes. He's not a homo." She slaps the sandals from his hand.

"I don't think your son wearing a girl's sandal classifies him as a *homo*."

"Fuck off," the woman retorts, dragging the poor child with her.

"Where's your dad?" I ask the boy.

"Home," he cries.

"Who the hell do you think you are? Don't talk to my son." She continues dragging him across the parking lot toward the beach. "His dad is good for nothing. He won't let me see my son. All he does is sleep with whores. He deserved what I did and what I'm going to do."

"Did you take him?"

The woman doesn't answer. I turn my attention toward the boy again. "Did she take you from your dad?"

"Shut up, bitch!" she yells, dragging him off the concrete onto the sand.

"She killed my dad," the boy whispers just loud enough for my hearing. "She's going to do the same to me."

Large blue eyes look into mine as he pleads for help. I move in front of her, blocking her path. "You're not going to hurt him," I warn.

"Get out of my way!"

I wrap my hand around the arm holding the boy in place, squeezing tight enough that she's forced to release her hold. She screams as the bones in her wrist begin to crack. "Go," I tell the boy.

He doesn't waste time. He turns, running to a small gas station not far away. "No!" she screams. "He has to die! We both do!"

I wrap my arms around her waist, pulling her close to me. This woman is in pain. She's a murderer, but then, so am I.

Moving faster than human eyes can track, I carry her to a parked police car with two officers inside. "This woman murdered her husband."

A young officer exits the car. "Did I understand you correctly?" he asks.

"Let me go!" the woman continues screaming.

"Look in her purse. You'll find her ID. She murdered her husband and was going to do the same to her son." I nod toward the gas station, where the boy took refuge. "He's in there. He'll corroborate the story."

The officer grabs her unbroken wrist, looking between the two of us. "Who are you?"

"A concerned citizen," I answer, sounding more like a superhero than the killer I am.

The second officer exits the car, heading straight toward me. I don't wait for more questions or interrogations. I move faster than they can track, disappearing before their eyes.

Crail, Scotland
2024

Where the small cottage once stood, now sits a grand three-story house. The farmland my family worked so hard to farm is covered in homes similar to the one in front of me. Any remnants of my familial home are gone, nothing more than memories cast in the wind.

I wipe the silent tears flowing from my eyes, as thoughts of what could've been flash to mind. If only I'd been normal. If only I had not been the reason my father died, none of this would've happened.

Instead, I've been on the run for two centuries, staying one step ahead of my captor and leaving a trail of death and destruction in my wake. I'm tired. I'm tired of killing. I'm tired of running. I'm tired of being a vampire. I'm tired of everything.

For the first time in a while, I allow thoughts of Thorne to enter my mind. Since escaping, thinking of him and our time together only brings sadness. I've avoided thinking of what could've been, instead focusing on survival.

"Captain Hawthorne Rex, I'm sorry," I whisper into the wind. For three centuries, I've passively searched for information on Thorne, finding not much in return. Today, that changes. Pulling my cell phone from my backpack, I book a flight to Charleston. The location where our ship was heading before Kragen took me. It's one of the few places I've avoided since escaping. That ends today.

charleston, south carolina

MODERN DAY

THE SMELL of humans permeates my nose, making me hungry. I haven't eaten for the past two weeks, partly on purpose and partly because of guilt. Walking through the city market is not the smartest activity for a hungry vampire, especially during tourist season. This is the third day I've been here. Being able to resist the urge to eat gives me hope in a future where I'm not a killer. However today, the sheer amount of people crammed into the narrow building is nearly overwhelming to my desires.

A woman who appears no older than me bumps into me, nearly knocking herself over in the process. "Excuse me," she says, turning toward me.

"No worries," I smile, making eye contact with her.

The smile on her face fades as something inside her sends a silent warning. Not every human can sense the danger I represent, but this woman does. She turns quickly, moving in the opposite direction.

I continue walking, sliding gracefully between the visitors. I watch as mothers and fathers push strollers of exhausted children through the crowded market. This is just the sort of place tourists flock to. Overpriced items imported from other countries, stamped with Charleston insignias, always draw a crowd.

The smell of sulfur catches my nose, bringing me to a stop in the middle of a crowd. The humans continue moving around me, giving me wide berth, no doubt sensing my energy.

Sulfur is one of those smells that triggers memories I would rather forget. A past I'd rather not think about. Especially here, surrounded by humans.

I find myself looking around, halfway expecting to see him. Where Kragen went, the smell of sulfur accompanied. I scour the area, searching for any sign of the man, hell, the creature, I've spent the past two hundred years hiding from.

I've stayed one step ahead of him since escaping. As horrible as it was, I have to give him credit. It was Kragen who turned me into the creature I am today, nothing more than a nightmare incarnate.

I continue walking, leaving the city market, and making my way closer to the water's edge. Sunset is my favorite time, and exploring the city I was headed toward all those years ago is something I've wanted to do since escaping...although, if I'm honest, I have other motives.

Charles Town, or Charleston as it's called now, would've been the first place Kragen looked after I left. It's the reason I've waited two hundred years to visit. The Charles Town I was bound for would've looked nothing like the tourist trap it is today. I try to picture Mama and my siblings exiting the ship into the town that would be their new home.

Memories of my brother Charles flood my mind, bringing the sadness that always accompanies his memory. He died never seeing his new home. He died, never understanding what happened to him. Maybe that was a blessing.

Standing on the battery, I lift my arms, allowing the wind to blow through the silky sleeves of my shirt. Sea water brings memories of home. "Be careful. I'd hate to have to save you," a voice says from behind. I turn, finding the source. A man a few inches taller than me has his hands shoved deep into his pockets and a wistful look on his face.

"I'm fine, thank you," I answer, returning to my view.

"Michael," the man says.

I turn back. "Excuse me?"

"Michael. That's my name."

"Oh." I laugh. "I thought you were confused for a moment."

"Ha! No. Just introducing myself." He moves to my side. "What are you looking at?"

"The wind," I answer, not sure I'm up for company.

He looks in my direction. "That would've been my first guess. Are you here with family?"

"Do you always ask random strangers so many questions, Michael?"

He shuffles back and forth. "I do, sorry." He shoves his hands back into his pockets. "My friends all got wasted and fell asleep at the hotel. I was bored and came for a walk." I don't respond, hoping to discourage his conversation. "Where are you from?"

I sigh before answering. Occasionally, humans are attracted to the energy of a vampire. Attracted to the danger they sense in me. "Scotland."

His eyes open wide. "I thought I heard a slight accent. I've always wanted to visit." He shuffles once more. "What brings you to Charleston?"

"I was hungry," I answer, hoping he'll lose interest.

He runs a hand through dark hair. "I was just about to grab something to eat. Would you like to join me?"

The insatiable thirst deep inside rumbles at his words. "Just the two of us?"

"Aye." He smiles with his word. "That is what they say, isn't it?"

"Aye, it is." I move closer toward him. As hungry as I am, I don't want to hurt this man. I don't want to hurt anyone ever again. I look into his eyes, focusing on the dark pupil in the middle. "Michael, you need to leave me alone. I am not who or what you think I am."

"Who are you," he whispers.

"I am death. Go, before you are my next victim."

Michael's eyes come back into focus. "I need to leave." His voice is monotone and robotic.

I turn, facing the sea and giving him time to return to reality. "Hey, listen," he stumbles. "I'm going to go." He backs away slowly, never taking his eyes off me. "It was really nice meeting you."

I don't respond as he leaves me alone on the river's edge. In the two hundred years I've been on the run, I learned many things. Compulsion was just one of them.

I turn, heading through the crowds and the city streets to the home I've rented during my time here. The rental listing advertised the home as a "vampire home," banking on the history of vampires in the city. Whatever their reason, it was enough to convince me to bite. I laugh at the irony of my thoughts.

The house is four stories high and narrow. Most of the older colonial-style homes fit the same mold: tall and narrow, with each floor hosting its own piazza. To be honest, I don't know why I chose such a large home to live in alone. Six bedrooms are much more than necessary for one person, especially for someone who doesn't sleep. I make my way to the third-level piazza and sit, overlooking the Ashley River a few blocks away.

Thoughts of my mother, raising my siblings alone

in a new country, overwhelm me. She was the strongest woman I ever met. I can't imagine how she survived.

Through the research I've done, I learned that after arriving in Charles Town, Mama worked tirelessly to support her family, never remarrying. Through the years, I've been able to find information on all of my siblings except Bertram and the baby. I'd like to think he survived, but I'll never know. There are records of Bertram arriving in Charles Town, but nothing about his life afterward. Over the years, I gave up, assuming he moved away or changed his name.

"I'm sorry I wasn't here, Mama," I whisper, remembering the day I was taken. Over the years since, I've avoided thinking too much about that day. The memories only bring pain. The phone shoved into my pocket vibrates, bringing me back to the present and away from my haunting past. On the screen is an address. One that I've been waiting all week to receive.

417 East Bay Street

"417 East Bay Street," I repeat the address out loud the private detective I hired sent out loud. Butterflies take flight in my stomach. A quick search on my phone tells me the address is less than three blocks away. "It's now or never, Elsie." I don't waste time walking. Leaping from the piazza, I'm in front of the Colonial Style home in less than a minute.

Chill bumps cover my skin at the thought of who

once owned this home. The man I've thought about for three hundred years.

The thick nautical rope-shaped woodwork surrounding the door shows that the people who built this home earned their money from the sea. This has to be it. I take a deep breath, moving up the walkway toward the narrow front porch.

"Hello?" a soft voice says from a chair in the corner. "This house isn't on the tour, sweetie."

"I'm not looking for a tour," I answer.

The woman stands, giving me a full glimpse of someone who looks to be in their late seventies. Her shoulders are slumped slightly, and glimpses of once dark hair peek through a head full of perfectly styled white curls. "If you're here looking for a room to rent, I don't have anything available at the moment."

I fight the urge to help the elderly woman walk. "You rent rooms?"

"Aye," she answers, giving me a slight hint of a familiar accent.

"Do you know when you might have one available?"

"Hmm. Tomorrow, I think. The couple in the honeymoon suite are leaving in the morning."

"I'll take it," I interrupt.

She smiles widely. "You want the honeymoon suite? Will your husband be joining you?"

"I'm not married. I'm more interested in the history of the home. The honeymoon suite is a bonus."

She works her way toward the door. "Francis Hawthorne," she says, holding her hand toward me.

My heart, or what's left of it, skips a beat at her name. "Elsie Abernathy. What time should I check in tomorrow?"

She sighs before answering. "Well, checkout is at eleven. I'm sure it'll take me a few hours to get the room back in shape. How does three o'clock sound?"

"It sounds perfect. Thank you."

"How long will you be staying?" she asks.

Turning back toward the heavy front door, I run my hand over the carved woodwork. "I'm not sure."

"The room is two hundred dollars a night during this time of year. I'm sorry to charge that much for a single young woman like yourself."

"It's not a problem," I interrupt. "I understand." I turn my attention back to the woodwork. "This is beautiful. Is it original to the house?"

"Aye, it is. My grandfather several generations back made his fortune on the sea. He used that money to build this house. It's been in our family for nearly three hundred years. Renting out the rooms is the only way I can afford the upkeep on it now."

"It's beautiful," I whisper.

"Thank you." She turns, heading through the heavy door. "Tomorrow, then?"

"Yes, ma'am. I'll be here at three o'clock." I turn, leaving the woman on her doorstep, and move toward the busy street.

In the time I've been a vampire, I've never forgotten the man who won my heart all those years ago. The man who I barely knew yet was willing to risk his life to save me.

Sadness fills me. It always does when his memory comes to mind. It's the main reason I've waited this long to discover his legacy. Over the years, I've searched randomly, never finding any substantial information. For the most part, any record of Captain Hawthorne Rex stopped not long after Kragen took me.

It doesn't take long to pack the meager belongings I traveled here with. I don't bring much with me when I travel. It makes it easier to leave quickly should the need arise.

Three o'clock comes much too slowly as I patiently wait on the bottom floor piazza. I watch as unsuspecting tourists pass the rental home, exploring the rich history of the city. The majority of them have no idea of the creatures that lurk in the darkness. Creatures like me. I could kill hundreds of them within seconds. A wet tear streams down my cheek at the thoughts filling my mind. Dark thoughts. Evil thoughts.

You're not that woman anymore, I remind myself. *You did what you had to do to survive.* The clock tower, several blocks away, chimes on the hour, letting me know it is exactly three. The time Ms. Hawthorne said the room would be ready. I stand, take a deep breath, and head toward the home.

I focus on moving at the same speed as the

humans surrounding me and blending in with the crowd. Five minutes later, I knock on the heavy wooden door.

The older woman opens the door, wearing a wide smile. "You did come back. I wasn't sure you would."

"Of course, I did. I can't wait to study the history of your home."

She steps away from the door, giving me room to enter. "I don't know how much history I can share that's not in the books, but I'll give it a try. I don't get much company other than guests. It'll be nice to have someone to talk to." She walks toward a small desk in the foyer. "Let's get you checked in."

I follow her, setting my small bag on the ground at my feet. Inside, the home is just what I imagined it to be. Pictures of ships, new and old, line the navy blue walls of the deep foyer. "This is beautiful."

"Thank you," she smiles, following my line of sight. "Most of the pictures are ships that members of my family have sailed throughout the years."

My eyes are drawn to a familiar-looking vessel. Instead of a photograph, it's a sketch of the ship that Thorne commanded—the ship where I was taken.

"What about this one?" I point to the picture.

"Hmm?" she sets down the paper she was holding and moves to my side. "Oh, that is the ship that started it all. It belonged to the man who built this house. Captain Rex."

I found him. I focus on keeping the energy buzzing

through my body still. "Captain Rex? What happened to him?"

"That's a good question," she answers. "Records show he made several trips between here and Scotland when he was very young. He married a young woman from Charles Town, my great-great-great-grandmother, built a small fortune, and had a son. After that, no one knows."

"What do you mean?"

Ms. Francis shrugs. "He went to sea one day and never returned."

"Was the ship sunk?"

"No, that's the strange part. He disappeared in the middle of the night. When the ship returned to port, he was never seen or heard from again. Most people speculated that he fell overboard or possibly jumped." My heart jumps into my throat at the thought of Thorne disappearing.

"That's horrible."

She takes a deep breath. "I imagine it was." She turns back toward the desk. "Now, let's get you checked in."

I spend the next few minutes sharing all of my information, or at least the information that I'm willing to share and get checked into Thorne's home.

Following the woman up the stairs, we pass photo after photo of different ships. "Here we are," she says, opening a door off the main hallway. Inside, I'm surprised at how lavishly the room is decorated. The four-poster bed looks antique, making me wonder if it's original to the home. Green velvet bedding covers the top, giving it a warm feeling. Wide plank boards cover the floor and are home to a thick rug that matches the bedding.

"Speaking of Captain Rex, this was the room he used when he lived here."

My heart stops. "Really? This very room?"

"Yes." She moves toward the headboard of the old bed, rubbing the wood gently. "This is the same bed he slept in. Not the same mattress, of course." She laughs at her words.

She moves toward an ancient wardrobe. "This is original to the room, along with that washstand." She points to a small table, holding an antique water basin. "There are quite a lot of items throughout the home that are original. Over the years, many things have broken or been destroyed. This room seems to hold the most."

"Thank you, Ms. Hawthorne."

"Call me Francis, please."

"Thank you, Francis."

She works her way toward the door. "Dinner will be served promptly at six o'clock. If you will not be eating, I ask that you tell me so that I don't overcook. Other than that, I'll leave you be." I watch the elderly woman close the door behind her and fight the tears that threaten to fall.

After all these years, I've found him. I finally found him.

food for thought

WORKING my way down the stairs, I touch every picture as I pass, longing to learn more about each one. I know without looking that there are five people besides Ms. Francis in the room below: two men, two women, and a child.

The smell of shrimp and grits fills my nose as I move toward the noisy dining room. "Miss Abernathy, welcome," Ms. Francis greets me as I enter the room. The table in the middle of the room is large enough to seat twenty guests. On the perimeter, several smaller tables are set, each holding a few people. "Sit wherever you like. I've prepared a low-country favorite. I hope you're not allergic to shrimp."

"I'm not," I lie. Actually, not a lie, just an omission. I haven't eaten food in nearly three hundred years. I sit at one of the smaller tables, and she sets a steaming bowl in front of me.

"This looks amazing."

"I'm glad. Eat up."

I slide the food around in the bowl, hoping to make it look like I've eaten. Moving faster than human eyes can track, I dump half of the contents into a trash can nearby. "Would you join me?" I ask my hostess.

"Are you sure?" she asks.

"Of course. I'd love to ask more questions and discover more history on the home and Captain Rex."

She giggles as she sits down. "That reminds me. I found an old book that you're welcome to borrow if you like. After you checked in earlier, I remembered I had a history of the ships that belonged to the Hawthorne Company. You're welcome to look through it."

I focus on keeping my expression calm. "I'd like that, thank you."

"You're welcome, dear. Not many people your age are interested in history. Especially history from the 18th century."

I smile at the irony. "No, I guess not."

She looks down, noticing my half-empty bowl. "Oh, how rude of me. Would you care for more?"

"No, thank you. I couldn't eat another bite. It was delicious."

"You know, I'm still finding items that were hidden around the house," she adds as she stands.

"Items? What kind of items?"

Francis shrugs. "You know. Journals, pictures, books...those kinds of things."

"Have you found anything from Captain Rex?"

She shakes her head. "No, can't say that I have. That would be interesting, though." I wait at my table, strategically moving the remaining food in my bowl around, and wait for the rest of the guests to leave. Thankfully, it doesn't take long. As soon as the last couple exits the room, I help Ms. Francis pick up the dishes.

"You don't need to help me, dear. I can do it."

"I don't mind. I could use the company."

"Aye, me, too." She laughs.

Over the years, I've met hundreds, even thousands of humans. In that number, I can count on one hand how many of them I've felt comfortable around. Ms. Francis is one of them. Her energy offers peace for a reason I can't explain.

"If you don't mind, after we clean up from dinner, I thought maybe you could give me some history on some of the photographs and drawings."

"I'd like that," she answers.

Returning the dining room to its original splendor doesn't take long. Heading into the kitchen, I find her washing dishes in the sink by hand. I move to her side, taking over the position of drying.

"How long have you lived here?" I ask.

"Near about eighty years. I was born in that dining room you just ate in."

"Really?"

She sets a wet plate on the counter. "Mama always

said the Hawthornes weren't very patient. I wouldn't wait until she got to the hospital and made an appearance early."

"You never changed your name?"

"No," she answers, picking the wet plate back up. "Never found anyone I was interested in. Back in my time if you didn't marry a man, you were thrown in a mental institution."

I turn, facing the elderly woman. "You didn't want to marry a man?"

She huffs. "No. Why would anyone want that?" Her eyes take on a faraway look. "I was in love once. It didn't work out."

"I'm sorry." I don't know why I'm apologizing.

"Me, too."

"Who will take over the house when you…"

Ms. Francis laughs. "You can say it. When I die? I'm old, but I'm not stupid. I won't be around forever." She sighs before continuing. "I don't have any direct descendants to pass it down to. There are a few distant nieces and nephews, but no one seems interested. I reckon when I'm gone, so will Hawthorne Mansion."

"I'm sorry to hear that. What if I could help?"

"Help? Don't take this the wrong way, but you're barely out of diapers. The upkeep is astronomical."

"Maybe I can find someone. Would you mind if I work on it?"

She hands the plate to me to dry. "Of course not. I'd appreciate the help."

Back in my room, I research every bit of information available on Hawthorne Mansion, finding barely anything. From what I can tell the name was changed from something different around a hundred years ago. Before that time, there is nothing stating the original name of the home.

Ms. Frances brought the book she found after dinner, and I have spent the last few hours reading through every bit of information and pouring over every photograph. I half expected to see an image of Thorne, disappointed there wasn't.

Remembering what she said about finding hidden items around the house, I slide the heavy bed away from the wall. Searching behind the wooden, frame, I hope to find a link to Thorne.

Finding nothing, I move toward the water basin, hoping to find something Ms. Francis missed. Again, I find nothing. I move toward the ancient wardrobe in the corner of the room. The top of the cabinet nearly touches the twelve-foot ceilings in the large bedroom. I run my hands down the wood, imagining Thorne doing the same. I open it, finding nothing more than extra linens. "Did you use this, Thorne?" I ask softly. "Did you store your clothes inside?"

Moving to the bottom of the cabinet, I run my hand along the creases of the wood. Tears form, thinking about Thorne and the future life that ended so suddenly. I pull a drawer full of embroidered pillow-cases out, hoping for some connection, finding nothing.

I carefully place the antique linens on the floor next to me, realizing something rattled inside the drawer.

Shaking the empty drawer, it rattles again. How is that possible? It's empty. I turn the drawer over in my hands, looking for something mechanical to be loose. I notice the corner of a piece of paper underneath the wood.

I pull on the corner, not sure what it's attached to. The corner breaks off in my fingers. "Shit," I whisper.

Carefully, I pry what looks like a false bottom off the drawer. As soon as the wood separates, a small leather-bound journal falls to the floor, spilling its contents.

I close my eyes, begging this to be something that belonged to Thorne. I take an unnecessary deep breath and open the cover. Inside, in beautiful script hand-writing are the words I've longed to see.

Property of Captain Hawthorne Rex

I can't hold in the tears. Three hundred years later, this is the closest I've been to him. I run my fingers over the letters, admiring the penmanship. I imagine him sitting at his desk in the captain's quarters, writing his fears, hurts, hopes, and dreams inside.

Climbing on top of the large bed, I bring the journal with me. Holding something of Thorne's after all these years feels surreal.

Carefully turning the pages, I read late into the

night. The pages are filled with short glimpses into his life as a captain. Most are about the weather or dangers of the coastline. I run my fingers across a drawing of a seagull. Each page is a replica of the last until something grabs my attention. Hastily scribbled on a page is the word *followed*. I turn the page, looking for clues, and find the mention again. This time he mentions that he didn't trust Smith, the man I remember as his first officer.

A few pages later, I see his name mentioned again.

Smith is a man who will do anything for money—even selling his soul to the devil.
I wonder how it will affect us?

"What did you suspect, Thorne?" I whisper, turning the page.

A ship is following us. Smith tries to deny any involvement, but I know they're there.
I don't know what it means for our vessel. I don't think they have good intentions.
Elsbeth continues to sleep.

I stare at my name written in his journal. "Elsbeth

continues to sleep," I say out loud, repeating his words about me. "I'm here, Thorne."

Turning the page, I realize I'm toward the end of his writings.

> They're coming. I can feel it. We're not safe, but there's nothing I can do.
>
> Elsbeth is awake, and my heart is grateful. My acushla.
>
> She is the most beautiful being on earth.
> I wonder if she knows
> what she does to me?
> I must protect her at all costs.

Tears flow at his admission. There was nothing beautiful about me during that time. I'd gone months without a bath, and my hair was full of lice and tangles. What could have been beautiful about that? I turn to the last entry.

> She's gone. He took her. The creature took her.
>
> I will not rest until I find her. No matter what I have to do, I will find you, Elsbeth Abernathy.

I close the journal, crying the tears I've held in for so

long. "I'm sorry, Thorne," I whisper into the pages. "I'm sorry I was never found." I cry for both of us.

A soft knock on the door brings me back to reality. "Elsie, dear. Are you okay?"

I wipe the tears from my stained face. "I'm fine, Ms. Francis. Just had a bad dream."

She's quiet so long, I'm convinced she's left. "If you're sure then. I thought I heard crying. Would you like a glass of milk to help you go back to sleep?"

"No, thank you."

"Good night," she says through the closed door.

"Good night," I answer.

I don't need shrimp and grits or milk. What I need is blood. It's been a while since I've eaten, and being surrounded by humans is making it more difficult. I carefully close the journal and place it in the drawer beside the bed.

Leaving through the window, I'm on Battery Street seconds later. I need to eat, but I refuse to harm anyone. I find a nearby bar full of people. Making my way inside, I focus on keeping my energy hidden.

It doesn't take long before someone bites.

"Hey, sexy. Are you alone?"

I turn, finding a middle-aged man who reeks of alcohol and sex. I smile. "Not anymore." I pat the empty stool next to me.

"Are you old enough to be in a bar?" he asks.

"What they don't know won't hurt them." I wink.

"Why don't you buy me a drink, and we'll see how old I really am?"

The man smiles, revealing a mouth full of yellow teeth. "That's a plan. I like them young anyway."

He raises a hand in the air. "Two shots." The bartender nods in his direction before bringing two small glasses of brown liquid to us. I fight the urge to roll my eyes at the cheap drink he just purchased. I down the glass in one gulp, slamming it on the bar in front of me.

"Damn, girl. Slow down a little. I don't want you too drunk to suck my dick."

I laugh at the irony. "That's not all I'm going to suck."

He raises his hand, ordering two more shots. I mimic my behavior from before, this time pretending to sway on my barstool. "Oh, my. Maybe you were right. I should've slowed down a little." I turn off the Scottish brogue that has been with me for three hundred years, turning it into the drunk Southern girl.

"Why don't we get out of here?"

"Not until you buy me one more drink."

He laughs, raising his hand in the air. I copy my movements from before, this time pretending to nearly fall off the stool. The man wraps his arm around me, pulling me away from the bar and toward the door. Once outside, I keep up the facade as he guides me into a small alleyway, not far from the main street.

"I need payment for those drinks."

I reach into my pocket, handing him a five-dollar bill.

"Five dollars? Those drinks are worth much more than that. I know the perfect way for you to repay me." He unzips his pants and pulls down the faded boxers he's wearing.

"I'd rather suck something else."

He smiles. "I thought you were joking." He lowers his pants to his ankles, exposing himself to anyone passing by.

Wrapping my hand around his neck, I turn him around, shoving his body into the brick of the building. A split second later, I'm on top of him, drinking the warmth from his neck. A deep sigh escapes as I fill my need with him.

Something moves not far away, stopping me from taking every last drop. I turn, seeing nothing there. The man in front of me is still breathing. "Shit, what are you doing, Elsie?" I ask no one. Releasing his body, I allow him to slide to the ground. He's breathing and will live another day.

I back away, leaving him another victim of a senseless crime. "Good girl," a voice whispers from the darkness.

My body goes rigid, hearing the familiar words Kragen said to me so many times. Did he find me? I sniff the air, expecting to be met with the scent of sulfur. Instead, I'm met with the now familiar smell of the city.

"You're imagining things, Elsie," I say aloud. "That's

a common saying," I try to reassure myself. Either way, I'm not going to wait around to find out. I turn, heading to the river edge, leaving the still alive body naked and alone. Usually, I'm more careful. With the combination of discovering the journal and being too hungry, I was reckless.

The fresh air of the river calms the turmoil slightly. I spend the rest of the night walking around the city and replaying Thorne's journal in my mind.

TEN

a visitor

"ELSIE, DEAR. BREAKFAST IS READY," Ms. Francis announces from the other side of the honeymoon suite door. "I hope you like waffles."

"My favorite," I lie. "I'll be right down." I listen as she knocks on the other guests' doors before heading back down the stairs.

After returning to the room, I've been curled into a corner, stuck deep in my self-pity, my fingers running mindlessly over the leather-bound journal. Through the years, I've often wondered if the feelings and emotions I have toward Thorne are nothing more than "puppy love." Thorne was the only man to ever talk to me—the only man to show me attention. Maybe the naive, sickly, demon-possessed girl fell for the first man with a pulse who looked at her.

As I touch the leather that Thorne held in his hands,

I know that's not the case. It was more than a schoolgirl crush. He felt it, too.

The sound of a door closing in the room next to me draws me back to the present. I carefully place the journal under my pillow and make sure there isn't any blood on my chin before exiting the room and heading downstairs.

"Good morning," I greet my only connection to Thorne. Ms. Francis is sitting at the table we shared yesterday with a plate in front of her and a full one on the opposite side.

"Good morning, Elsie. I took the liberty of making you a plate. I hope you don't mind."

"Not at all, thank you." I quickly begin moving the food around on my plate, focusing on holding back the sadness that I carried with me this morning.

"Both guests are checking out this morning, so it may be just the two of us for a few days. I hope that doesn't bother you," Ms. Francis says, taking a bite of eggs. She smiles, showing a dimple on the side of her cheek, and for a brief moment, I see a hint of her ancestor.

"Of course not. But please don't feel like you have to make meals for me. I'll just grab something in town."

"Hosh posh," she scolds. "You're a paying guest, and all of my paying guests receive meals. It's part of the service."

"You're too kind."

She laughs deeply. "There are some who would

disagree." I manage to move the food around enough that it appears I ate part of the breakfast.

While Francis performs the business aspect of checking the rest of the guests out, I clean the remaining food from the meal, taking the dishes into the kitchen.

Knowing the history of Charleston and the homes in the area, I know this room isn't original to the home. Still, my mind plays images of Thorne moving around the room…sitting at the small table next to the fireplace, picking up his son, and bouncing him on his knee.

Overwhelming sadness fills me at the thought of where our lives turned. At least he had a family and hopefully, a chance at happiness. Filling the sink with warm water, I mindlessly wash the dishes. It doesn't take long before the kitchen is clean, and the evidence of breakfast is put away.

"Did you do all of this?" Ms. Francis asks from behind me.

I turn, facing the elderly woman. "I did. I hope you don't mind."

"Mind? Never. Thank you."

"I thought maybe you could give me a history lesson on your family and the home."

She props her hands on her hips with a smile. "Well, since you took my job away, that sounds perfect. I need to clean the empty rooms first."

"I'll help you," I interrupt. "We can talk while we work."

"I couldn't ask you to do that," she retorts.

"You didn't. I'm volunteering. Consider it an exchange for your knowledge." I pull off the apron I'm wearing and prop my hands on my hips, copying her stance.

"You're not going to take no for an answer, are you?"

"You're figuring me out, Ms. Francis." I smile in return, motioning toward the door. "After you."

"This bedroom would have been the nursery originally," she says, leading me into a smaller bedroom in the back of the house. "All of the children would've been housed in this room until they were older." She moves toward a door in the back. "This would've been their nanny's room. Now it's a bathroom."

"All of the children in one room?" I think back to my siblings and how we shared one bed.

"Yes. Infant to teen. The other rooms would be kept as guest rooms. Back in those days, people didn't stop in for just a day. If you had a visitor, they might stay a week or even a month." We strip the bed of linens, piling them on the floor next to the door. "This was my room when I was young." She stops, looking around the room, clearly stuck in a memory.

"When the house was built, was this room meant to be the nursery?"

She huffs a short laugh. "Probably, but I wouldn't

know that answer for sure. However, we do know that Captain Rex only had one son, which explains why this room is so small. Until his wife remarried, he would have had it to himself."

"She remarried?" I'm not sure why that surprises me.

"Aye. It was customary for women to be married during those times. After mourning the death of her husband, she married a merchant from town." She moves toward a small dresser in the corner. "This piece is original to the room. My grandmother once told me it was made from the wood of Captain Rex's ship."

"It's beautiful."

"Aye, it is."

"What do you think happened to him, to Captain Rex?"

Francis sighs. "I don't know that anyone will ever know. It's rather sad if you think about it. My grandmother passed down stories of him throughout the years. Stories told to her by her grandfather. It was said he was a cold, bitter man."

I think back to the Thorne I knew. He was kind, gentle, and anything but bitter. "I think we all have more going on inside than we want the world to know."

Francis's laugh fills the room. "That's the statement of the year, dear girl." She moves to the clean linens we carried upstairs. "Do you mind helping me put these on? A guest is checking in this afternoon, and I want him to have this room."

"I thought you said we would be alone for a few days."

"Aye, I did. But through the magic of the internets, we have a guest coming today."

I smile at her attempt to sound technological while grabbing the sheets. In the time she tucks one corner in, I have the other three done and the top sheet in place. It doesn't take long to clean the rest of the room. While dusting, she gives me the history of each item and its significance to both Charleston and family history.

We're just about finished with the second bedroom when a feeling I haven't felt in a while threatens to overtake me. There's a vampire near—an energy I don't recognize.

"What's wrong, Elsie?" Ms. Francis asks, sensing my sudden change.

I clear my throat. "Nothing." I plaster a fake smile across my face. "I'm not feeling well after breakfast. Would you mind if I go and lie down?"

"Of course not. Our guest should be arriving soon. Get some rest, and thank you for your help."

I excuse myself and move across the hallway to the room I'm occupying. The feeling continues to grow. Shit. It's not Kragen's energy, but it somehow feels familiar. Could it be one of the creatures from his crew?

Grabbing the journal from its hiding spot, I exit the house before Ms. Francis registers movement. Once outside, I'm at the edge of the water less than a second later. I hold the journal to my chest, the last remaining connection I have to Thorne.

The energy continues to grow. Whoever it belongs to is strong and nearly as old as me. I turn, not sure what to expect, finding no one.

"Not all vampires are bad," I remind myself. "Not everyone is Kragen." My calming mantra has helped throughout the years. I've met others like me in the two hundred years since I escaped. Most were nothing more than sadistic killers. A few were passive and less threatening.

I turn back toward the river and run head first into the energy. Standing in front of me is a vampire. He's tall with a head full of dark curls and grey eyes, wearing a face I would recognize in a sea of millions.

"Thorne?" I whisper, not trusting my voice.

"Aye," he answers with a smile. "It's me, my love."

The wind is swept from my chest, and the world around me falls into blackness. I never thought it was possible for a vampire to pass out, yet here we are.

My eyes open to the familiar surroundings of the honeymoon suite. How did I get here? I jump from bed, not sure what's going on. Did I imagine that? Did I dream that? That's ridiculous, vampires can't sleep, let alone dream. I run downstairs, nearly slamming into Ms. Francis as she exits the sitting room.

"Oh, my. Elsie, are you all right?"

"Did you see anyone?"

"Other than you and our departed guests, no." She

wrinkles her forehead. "Are you sure you're all right, dear?"

I close my eyes. What the hell is wrong with me? Being here, in his home, is making me insane. "I'm okay. I'm afraid I'm going to have to check out today. I'll pay you two weeks' rent for the room. I can't be here any longer."

Sadness forms in her eyes, and I immediately feel guilty. "If you're sure. At least let me make you something to eat first. Our new guest should be arriving soon."

"No, that's not necessary." I wrap my arm through hers and pull her close. "Thank you for everything, Ms. Francis. I'm going to pack my things."

Back in the room, it doesn't take long to pack the few items I brought with me. Running my fingers over each piece of furniture and fabric, memorizing every fiber, smell, and texture, I realize it's time to let go of my obsession. Thorne died never knowing what happened to you. It's apparent from the journal he never got over that. Neither of us did.

Now, I'm imagining him in front of me. I focus on blocking any energy and masking my own as I exit the honeymoon suite and make my way downstairs. Ms. Francis is talking to someone, which means her new guest has arrived. Against my better judgment, I wait in the foyer to tell her goodbye. The old Elsie would have left without another word, but this is different. *She* is different.

"Right this way," she says, leading someone from the desk she uses for check-in. The man who follows behind is the same man from the banks of the river. The man I've been searching for...Thorne.

"Oh, Elsie, you're still here. This is our new guest, Thorne Smith." She motions to the man behind her. "Such a strong name, and one I've never heard before."

"Hello, Elsie," he greets me.

I stare at the man who's haunted my thoughts for centuries. "Hello, Thorne." My voice is no louder than a whisper. "Is it really you?"

"Aye, it is, acushla." Hearing his familiar name for me covers my skin with chill bumps.

Ms. Francis looks between the two of us. "You two know each other? How unusual is that?"

"Elsie is someone I've been searching for...for a very long time."

"Looks like you found her," she adds. "Oh, wait. I've seen some of those movies on cable. You're not a stalker or anything, are you?"

"Nothing like that," he answers. He turns his attention back toward me. "You're even more beautiful than I remember."

I've dreamed of this moment. I've imagined it thousands of times. It helped me to survive...gave me the strength to escape and brought me here. Suddenly, face-to-face with the only man I've ever loved, words fail me. The conversations that played through my head are gone, leaving me in shock and confusion.

"How?" I whisper. "How is this possible?"

"I can see you two have some catching up to do," Ms. Francis interrupts. "Why don't I carry your bag to your room, and you two do some catching up? The piazza is beautiful this time of day and shouldn't be too hot yet."

She takes the bags from both of our hands as we continue to stare at each other. Grey eyes search every inch of my face as the two of us refuse to release each other from our gazes.

"Okay, then," she continues. "The piazza is just through those windows." She nudges me toward two large windows that open onto the long porch.

three hundred years

SOMEHOW, we end up on the piazza without any recollection of moving from the foyer. I can't take my eyes off the man in front of me. Together, we sit on a large settee, overlooking the colorful backyard.

"How are you here?" I finally gain the courage to repeat.

Thorne looks down before speaking. "Unmask your energy, and feel mine. Then you'll know."

I do as he suggests, reaching for the energy of the man in front of me. I'm instantly met with the same energy I felt earlier. "Oh, my God. You're a vampire. That was you I saw earlier. I didn't imagine it."

"Aye."

"Kragen?"

He shakes his head, stopping the anger from forming. "It wasn't Kragen. It was my choice."

"Your choice? Why?"

"Because it was the only way to find you."

"You..." I stutter. "You willingly changed yourself into a vampire to find me?" The reality of his words hit me. "What the hell were you thinking?" I stand from the settee and move toward the edge of the piazza. "You had a family. You had a wife and a child, and you," I motion to the building surrounding us, "you had a home that you built."

He stands, matching my energy. "You're right, I had all of that, but I didn't have you."

"How could you do that to her? How could you do that to them?"

He sighs. "I was a horrible husband and a subpar father. My wife hated me, and I can't blame her. She was forced to marry me because the man she loved wasn't of her stature."

"He was a merchant," I interrupt, remembering Francis's words from earlier.

"Aye. Her father refused to let them marry. It was him that she loved, not me. I made sure she would be taken care of for the rest of her life. I gave her every penny I had along with this house and the blessing to marry who she truly loved. She gave me her blessing to do what I needed to do. She understood."

"She knew what you were doing? That you were planning on becoming a vampire?"

He closes his eyes. "Aye. It turned out to be the best thing for both of us."

"Francis is your great-great-great-granddaughter."

"I know," he whispers. "I've watched her off and on for many years."

I fight to keep the tears forming in my eyes from sliding down my cheeks. "Why did you keep yourself hidden from me?" My words feel selfish, leaving my lips.

His gaze softens, sensing my turmoil. "I never stopped searching. I came close to finding you several times, yet you managed to stay one step ahead of me. I never gave up on you. I *will* never give up on you."

Losing the battle with my tears, they stream down my face, making me feel weak. Something I haven't felt in a very long time.

"I'm so sorry, Elsie. I should've stopped him that day. I was a coward, and it's something I've regretted ever since."

"You survived. That's not being a coward. You brought my family safely here and helped them when no one else would. For that, I thank you. If you had died that day, they would've too."

He closes his eyes at my words. "It doesn't make it any easier. Three hundred years have passed since I saw him take you. For three hundred years, I've replayed that image in my mind, thinking of the things I should've done."

"You did what you had to do—live. I did what I had to do—survive." I wipe the stains from my cheeks. "How did you find me?"

One side of Thorne's mouth lifts higher than the

other. "I come to Charleston every few months to check on Francis."

"She acted like she didn't know you."

"Aye, she doesn't. I stay in the background, never allowing her to see me."

"Until now," I interrupt. "Why?"

"I sensed you. I knew you were here and where you were."

"In your home." I laugh. "I was looking for something to connect me to you."

"You found it." His voice is soft as his eyes peer into mine. "I'm not going anywhere."

I step closer, giving in to the desire of my heart instead of my head. Thorne's energy matches mine. His desire is evident on his face.

"Everything okay in here?" Ms. Francis interrupts. Thorne steps back, putting distance between the two of us.

"Just catching up," he says. "You were right. This piazza is lovely this time of year."

She claps her hands. "I agree." She turns toward me. "Elsie, dear. I took the liberty of putting your bag back in the honeymoon suite. Mr. Smith, yours is in the room opposite hers. I do hope that's all right."

"That sounds perfect," he answers with a warm smile.

"How about a nice bowl of gumbo for lunch? I have some leftovers that are begging to be eaten."

I look at the vampire in front of me. "That would be lovely."

"It sounds perfect," he agrees. "Thank you, Miss Hawthorne."

"Oh, please. Call me Francis." She looks between the two of us. "I think you two are going to be my favorite guests so far." She turns, disappearing into the house.

"It seems we're being beckoned for lunch," Thorne says, holding his arm toward me. "Shall we?"

I don't know whether to attack him, kiss him, or wrap my arm through his. I choose the latter, hooking my arm through his, and allowing him to lead me back through the windows into the sitting room.

"We have much to talk about," I whisper loud enough for his ears only as we join Ms. Francis at the table. She's mysteriously placed three already warm bowls of gumbo on the table and is waiting for our return. He nods in response.

I fight the urge to stare at the man that I've dreamed about for centuries. His features are more pronounced than I remember. Strong cheekbones accentuate his angular face. The once dark hair that stayed tied at his neck is now short and wavy, giving him a more modern look. Deep grey eyes hold the same intensity I remember from centuries ago. Sitting at the dining room table of his home in Charleston feels surreal.

"Tell me about yourself, Thorne," Francis interrupts.

He huffs a laugh. "There isn't much to tell. My family comes from Upstate. I love to visit Charleston whenever I can. The history is amazing here."

"That's true," she agrees. "It's what brought Elsie here, too." She smiles at me. "How do you two know each other?" Ms. Francis is ruthless with her questioning.

"We know each other from..." he stumbles over his words.

"From college," I interrupt. "We have a few classes together. Neither of us realized we were staying in the same city during spring break."

Francis laughs. "Is that so?"

"Yes, ma'am," he answers, pulling on a Southern drawl. "We met in history class, ironically." Thorne takes a small sip of the gumbo. I've never seen a vampire eat food before.

"Seems you two are a good match." She smiles once more. "I'm going after more cornbread. Would anyone else care for a piece?"

"No, thank you," we say in unison. I watch her leave the room before moving vampire speed to the trash and pouring part of my meal out. I'm back in my seat well before she enters the room carrying a slice of brown cake.

"Would you like more, Elsie?"

I pat my stomach for dramatic effect. "No, thank you. I'm stuffed."

"Why don't we go for a walk?" Thorne asks after we help Ms. Francis clean the dishes from lunch.

"I'd like that." We exit the house, moving toward the river. We have three hundred years of history to discover, but we walk in silence.

"Tell me about your life," I ask as we approach the moving water. "How did you become a vampire?"

We find a bench near the water's edge, sitting side by side. "I asked."

"You asked?" I repeat his words.

"If Kragen didn't change you, who did?"

Thorne runs a hand through his messy curls. "After arriving here, my shipping company was in charge of exchanging goods with the city of New Orleans. I made the trip once a year, and each time I would search for someone who held the answer to my desires. It was on one of those trips that I met him."

"A vampire?"

"Aye, a vampire. He wasn't like the ones who took you. He was normal, or at least as normal as a vampire can be."

"What do you mean by normal?"

"I mean, he didn't kill humans for sport. He didn't drink their blood. He was a businessman and a member of New Orleans society."

How is that possible? "If he didn't drink human blood, how did he survive?"

"Goat blood mostly, and an occasional small animal if no goats are available."

I stare at Thorne, not sure if I heard him correctly. "He drank goat's blood?"

"Aye. As I do now."

I sniff his direction. "That's why you smell different."

Thorne laughs. "Maybe. I never thought about it."

"Does the goat's blood make you weak?"

"No," he answers. "I'm as strong as a three-hundred-year-old vampire should be."

"Is your maker still alive?"

Thorne looks down. "No. He died protecting someone who he loved very much. His name was Viktor, and he was a great man. I hadn't spoken to him for the last fifty years or so. However, there was no anger or bitterness between us. We simply were living our own lives."

"I'm sorry," I confess.

"Aye, me, too. He was not only my maker, he was my friend."

"He agreed to change you into a vampire to find me?"

"Aye. It took several years of convincing, but he relented. I think it was the story of true love that changed his mind in the end." Butterflies take flight with his words. "It was during one of those deliveries that I left the ship and never returned home."

"You've only had goat's blood since turning?"

"Aye...and an occasional cat."

"Can you teach me how to do that?" Tears escape my eyes. "I don't want to kill anymore."

"Aye. I can." Thorne wipes a tear from my cheek. The warmth of his hand against my skin is almost overwhelming. "You are still the most beautiful creature I've ever seen. I would do everything over again for this moment, here with you."

My eyes close with his words. "After Kragen took me, it was the memory of you that kept me alive. Living with him was..." I pause, not sure how much to say. "Living with him was a nightmare."

Thorne's hand slides down my arm to my hand, pulling it tight into his, offering strength to continue. "Kragen used me in *every* form of the word. He would starve me to near death, only to feed me enough blood to bring me back to life, and begin the torture again. He got off on the pain he caused." The energy coming from Thorne changes as I speak.

"I was his plaything—his toy. When he was bored, the others would take their turns. I was nothing more than an object for entertainment and fun." I sigh before continuing. "Through the years, I lost track of time. Being deprived of sunlight and nourishment took a toll on my body and left me nothing more than a shell of my former self. One of his crew members took pity on me and would secretly bring me blood. I used him. I toiled with his affection while gaining strength every day." I wipe another tear from the memory. "I used him like they'd used me for all those years. He was young and naive and thought we were in love."

"What happened to him?"

"He died." I clear my throat at the memory. "He was murdered when I escaped." I close my eyes, reliving Elliot's death.

Thorne squeezes my hand. "I can't imagine what you've been through. The thought of it..." He doesn't finish his statement. He stands, moving closer to the water. Anger rolls off him. "I'm so sorry, Elsbeth. I should've been there for you."

"It's not your fault," I remind him.

"Aye, directly it wasn't, but I'm the one who hired Smith. I put my trust in him. He was the one who contacted them and told them about you," he confesses. "I discovered years later that he sent a message through one of Kragen's men and told them there was a sick young girl on board. He sold you to repay a debt."

I stare at Thorne, not sure I heard him correctly. "That son of a bitch traded my life for a debt?" It's my turn to be angry.

"Aye. I'm sorry, Elsie."

"How did he die?"

"I killed him," Thorne answers softly. "He suffered first."

Hearing that the human who sold me to vampires to repay a debt died violently shouldn't bring comfort, but it does. "Good."

"I've searched for centuries for you. Always one step behind…one day away. Even Viktor, with all of his knowledge and power, wasn't able to find Kragen or you. Bloody bastard."

"He still searches for me." My words draw his attention back to my face. "After all these years, he still searches," I repeat. "It's why I keep moving. Why I never stay anywhere long enough to be found."

"Until now. I've finally found you."

"Aye," I answer, stepping inches in front of him. "You found me."

Thorne's eyes search mine before his large hands cup each cheek. "I love you, Elsbeth Abernathy. I've loved you since the first time you stole my water to wash the shite off your hands, and I've never stopped."

Kissing Thorne is something I've dreamed about for three hundred years. Standing here, staring into his eyes, I do something young Elsie would've never done. I crash my lips into his, not wanting to wait another minute.

Thorne reacts instantly, pulling me even closer until there's no space between the two of us. He separates my lips with his tongue, and the sensation of our tongues colliding nearly sends me over the edge.

I fight the urge to undress him on the riverbank when a sensation I've only felt one other time hits me, making me pull away quickly.

"Do you feel that?" I ask, out of breath.

Thorne turns his nose to the sky. "Shit," he whispers.

"What is it?"

"It's not a what. It's a who," he answers, stepping away from me.

Turning toward the source, I feel something I've only experienced once before. A young woman is leaning against a tree with her foot propped on the trunk and her arms crossed in front of her chest. Her hair is a mixture of bright pink and blonde. Something about her reminds me of a rockstar from the '80s. "Hi!" She waves.

"Do you know her?"

"I can hear you," she interrupts, moving closer. "My name is Luna." She holds a hand toward me. I shake it, not sure what else to do.

"What are you?" I ask, staring into bright green eyes.

"You didn't tell her?" she asks Thorne. "I'm not surprised." She punches him on the shoulder.

"Luna, this is Elsbeth," Thorne answers. Her eyes grow large with my name.

"Elsbeth? THE Elsbeth?"

Thorne sighs. "Elsbeth, this is Luna. She's my pet werewolf."

"Werewolf?" I stare at the girl in front of me, not sure what else to say.

"I prefer the term lycanthrope."

family and love

"LUNA? WHY ARE YOU HERE?" Thorne asks the young girl.

"I'm here to keep an eye on you. Topher insisted that you needed a babysitter, and I was tasked with the job." She wrinkles her forehead. "I believe we've had this conversation many times. I'm not sure why you suddenly don't remember."

"I don't need a babysitter. I told your Alpha I would never do anything to interfere with the peace between our groups, and I mean that."

I step back, staring at the duo in front of me. "What the hell are you two talking about? Alpha? Peace between groups?" I haven't felt this lost in several hundred years.

"You haven't been around many lycan, have you?"

"You're the second one I've met," I answer truthfully. "Why does her Alpha think that you need a babysitter?" I ask Thorne.

He rocks back and forth on his feet. "Because I threatened to expose them if they didn't help find you."

Luna crosses her arms and glares at the vampire in front of me. "Tell her what else," she warns.

"I may have threatened to run down Bourbon Street naked during Mardi Gras."

I can't control the laughter that erupts. "What purpose would that have served?"

He scuffs the dirt in front of him. "It was dumb. I was desperate. Desperate men do desperate things."

"Yep. That's why you're stuck with me," Luna agrees.

"No offense, Luna. You're young and inexperienced. I could rip your neck from your body before you even noticed I moved," Thorne warns, staring the young lycan down. "He must not be too worried about me if he sent someone so young and inexperienced."

"I'm here as an annoying companion. Think of me as the chihuahua that can take down a pit bull if she's backed into a corner."

"Tell your Alpha, I've found her. I'm not going to do anything stupid."

Luna turns her attention toward me. "You're Elsbeth?" she asks once more.

"Aye."

"You're even more beautiful than I imagined. How

have you lived this long and only known one lycanthrope?"

"It's a long story."

She huffs a laugh. "I'm here for the long haul. Looks like we have plenty of time." She turns toward Thorne's former home. "Is this where we're staying?"

"No, it's where Elsbeth and I are staying. You're on your own."

Luna pulls a phone in front of her face. Several minutes and taps later, she looks up with a smile. "Seems there was one room available. Not anymore. I'm going to go check in."

I watch as the young lycanthrope heads toward the home that Thorne built. "This is going to be interesting."

"I'm sorry, Elsbeth. I didn't realize my idle threats would end with me having a wolf babysitter for the long haul."

I wrap my arm through his and pull him toward the house. "Come on. We need to make sure she doesn't scare Francis."

We enter the house to find Francis and Luna embracing like old friends. "We have a new guest," Francis exclaims, pulling away from the lycanthrope.

"We met," I answer for the two of us.

"Luna's a lycan," Francis says, staring at the two of us.

"What?" I ask, not sure I understood her words correctly.

Francis laughs. "She's a werewolf."

Luna wraps one arm around Francis's shoulders. "She's right. I'm a wolf."

"When are you two going to tell me that you're vampires?" Francis's words stop me in my tracks. I stare at the woman, not sure I heard her correctly.

"What do you mean?" I ask.

"I may be old, but I'm not dumb. Now," she props her hands on her hips, "who's going to tell me what the hell is going on? It's not a normal Monday to have two vampires and a lycan in your home. That's usually more of a weekend thing." She laughs as she speaks.

Thorne and I stare at our host, not sure what to say. "Come into the sitting room, and I'll explain," Luna says, pulling Francis with her. "You two coming?" she asks.

The look on Thorne's face mirrors my own. I don't know whether to run or join them for tea. Thorne laces his fingers through mine, and we enter the room, staying close to the door. "What makes you think we're vampires?" I ask after a few minutes of awkward silence.

"For starters, you don't eat human food. I've seen you try and found evidence in the trash can of what you don't eat. Then there's this." She picks up a newspaper at her side, reading the headline out loud.

"Man found nearly drained of blood outside local nightclub."

"I'm guessing that was you, Elsie." I clear my throat, not sure how to answer.

"Are you afraid?" Thorne asks.

"Of you two? No. I've always been a bit sensitive to things other than the usual. I've known for a very long time that there are other creatures besides humans in this world. I just never thought I would house three of them in my home at once. I can't explain how I know, but I know neither of you is a threat to me. However, I would love to hear the full story of who you are to each other."

"Ooo, me. Pick me! Pick me!" Luna waves her hand from the other end of the couch.

"Nothing personal, dear. I think it might be better coming from one of them," Francis says.

Thorne and I share a look. I know without asking, he's unsure if he should tell her who he really is.

I take a deep breath. "You're right. We are vampires, and the attack on the man at the nightclub was me." I turn toward my fellow vampire. "Thorne had nothing to do with it. I was the one who injured him."

Francis waves the paper toward me. "From what this says, he was not a model citizen anyway. After recuperating, he's being arrested and charged with an entire list of crimes, stemming from sexual assault to robbery. Looks like you did everyone a favor with that one."

She stands, moving toward one of the pictures I asked her about the first day. It's a picture of a ship very similar to the one Thorne captained. She takes it off the wall, holding it toward me. "I'm guessing by your questions about the history of the home and Captain Rex, you are from that period. Did you know him? Did you know my ancestor? Is that why you're here?"

I'm not sure how to answer her questions. Thankfully, I don't have to. Thorne moves toward the couch, sitting on a chair near his great-great-great-granddaughter.

"Francis, I don't know how to say this, so I'm just going to say it. *I* am Captain Hawthorne Rex, and I built this home many years ago for my son and wife."

Francis stares into the young face of her ancestor. "How is that possible?" Her voice is no louder than a whisper.

"You are right. I am a vampire. I was turned nearly three hundred years ago. It was my choice."

"I...I don't know what to say," she admits.

"You don't have to say anything," Thorne answers. "I'm not here for anything other than to check on you and to find Elsie."

"Check on me?"

"Aye. It's something I've done since you were born. Always near, never seen. Just out of reach of human attention and eyes."

A tear streams down Francis's cheek. "You're my grandfather?"

"Several times back, aye. I'm so proud of you, Francis." I smile at his words. "You are an amazing woman."

"Thank you," she whispers, wiping a tear. "You're not related to me somehow, are you?" she asks me with a smile.

"No," I answer. "At least, I don't think so." Thorne nods, giving me permission to tell our story.

"My family and I set sail from Scotland, headed to Charles Town in the early 1700s. My father had recently died, and my mother wasn't able to support our large family on her own. I was considered...unmarriable at that time, so the burden fell strictly on her."

"Unmarriable?" she asks, wrinkling her forehead.

"I had epilepsy. At that time, no one really knew what it was. I was said to be demon-possessed and unable to bear children for that reason. No one in my village wanted a young woman who was prone to uncontrollable shaking and unable to provide an heir. For that reason, my mother had no choice but to leave."

"Did she have a job here?" Luna asks, suddenly interested in my story.

"Aye," I answer. "Mama used the last of our money to purchase tickets to bring us to America." I huff a laugh at the memory. "We were so poor, we shared two pairs of shoes between all of the children." Thorne looks down as I speak. Clearly, he's remembering the poor, sick girl from long ago.

"Captain Rex was the captain of your ship?" Francis puts the pieces together.

"Aye, I was. It was there that we met. I caught her

washing her shite-covered hands in my drinking water."

Luna and Francis share a laugh at the memory. "In my defense, I didn't realize the water belonged to the captain."

"That doesn't help this story," he adds.

"How did you become a vampire?" Luna asks.

I sigh before speaking. "I had a seizure, one that incapacitated me. Thorne took care of me. He allowed me to stay in the captain's quarters, made sure my family was able to eat, and it was then that I fell in love with him." I feel red cover my cheeks at my admission. "It was during that time that *he* found us."

"Who found you?" Francis asks.

"Kragen," Thorne answers. "My first officer was…"

"An asshole?" Luna fills in the blank.

"Aye, an asshole. In order to repay a debt to Kragen, he sold information about Elsie to one of Kragen's men. He told them there was a sick young lady aboard our ship, selling her in payment for his debt."

"They caught up with us not long into our journey," I continue. "Kragen boarded the ship and threatened to kill every soul on board if I didn't go with him." I wipe a stray tear. "He killed my brother to prove his point."

"You went with him to save your family?" Luna says. Her voice is no louder than a whisper.

"I had no choice."

"I'm so sorry, Elsie," Francis says. She turns toward Thorne. "I'm sorry for both of you."

"How did you get away?" Luna asks.

"Without going into detail, I waited for the perfect time and escaped. I've been on the run ever since."

"You mean he's still after you?" Francis asks.

"Aye. He's never stopped looking for the one who got away." Anger radiates from Thorne. I turn toward the ship captain. "There was nothing you could do, Thorne. You need to accept that." He stands, moving across the room.

"She's right," Francis adds. "You had to get them to safety. Without you, they all would've died." She moves behind him, laying her head on his forearm. "Without you, I wouldn't be here."

"God, this story is much more interesting and gut-wrenching than I could've ever imagined. No wonder you acted like a fool in New Orleans. I can't say that I blame you. I don't think you need a babysitter, I think you need an army," Luna announces, standing from the couch.

"An army?" I ask.

"How else are we going to fight Kragen?"

"Luna, you don't know this guy. He's one of the strongest vampires in existence. He's not going to just give up and go home. He's been pursuing me for two hundred years. He's not like me. Hell, he's not like Thorne or, for that matter, any of the vampires you know. He's ruthless, deadly, and a cold-blooded killer, and will stop at nothing to get what he wants. I've already been here too long. I've put you all in danger by staying as long as I have."

"You're not leaving, are you?" Francis asks.

"I don't have a choice. I won't put you in more danger."

Luna crosses her arms across her chest. "You don't need to go anywhere. There is an entire army of lycan that will stand at your side. I'm sure I can wrestle up a few vampires if needed. Some of them are decent."

"No. I won't endanger anyone else's life. Thank you for the offer, but I must go."

"I'm coming with you," Thorne announces. "I refuse to lose you again."

"And where he goes, I go," Luna answers. "Babysitting duties." She winks at the two of us.

Francis looks between the three of us. "Well, I'm not staying here by myself."

"You don't understand. He doesn't care who or how many people he has to go through. He doesn't think like everyone else."

"We have to try, Elsie," Thorne agrees. "We have to try."

I stare at the people in front of me, not sure what to think. For three hundred years, I've been alone, staying hidden in the background, secretly searching for information on Thorne and just out of reach of Kragen. Now, three people are willing to risk their lives for me. I don't know whether to be grateful or terrified.

"I'm going to call Topher. He'll know who to

contact here in Charleston." Luna pulls out her phone and moves into the foyer.

"What can I do?" Francis asks.

"You can stay safe," Thorne answers. "This isn't something that humans should be involved in. We have no idea what Kragen will do."

"Why is he so obsessed with you?" Francis asks. "Why not just admit defeat and let you go?"

I sit on the overstuffed couch, pulling my legs beside me. "I've wondered that a lot through the years. The only feasible answer I can come up with is that it's because I escaped. I survived. Kragen is a narcissistic asshole who dominates everyone around him. It took me a hundred years, but I escaped. I'm the one that got away."

"It seems to me he'd lose interest after all this time," she adds. On cue, the doorbell rings, making the hairs on my arm stand at attention. "Oh, my. Are we expecting anyone?"

"I'll get it!" Luna announces from the other room. "It's probably the cavalry."

Reaching out my energy, I can tell the person on the other side of the door is like her, a lycanthrope. I move behind her at vampire speed.

Luna opens the door, revealing a man not much older than her. He's tall, thin, and is the host of a head full of coal black hair. Bright green eyes take in every inch of our resident wolf. "Luna?" he asks with a smile.

"That's me! You got here quick."

"Yeah, I was in the neighborhood. My Alpha didn't give me any information other than an address and a name." He looks past Luna at the three of us. "You two are vampires? And you're…"

"Human," Francis answers with a wave.

"What's going on?"

Thorne moves toward the young lycanthrope, offering his hand to shake. "Thorne. It's a pleasure to meet you."

"Micah," he answers.

"We would like to meet with your Alpha."

Micah looks around the group. "Why?"

"That's something we'd rather share with him for right now. Please don't take offense to that."

The lycanthrope shifts from foot to foot. "I will ask him to set up a meeting."

"Thank you," Luna answers. "My Alpha spoke very highly of him."

"I'll be in touch." Micah turns, leaving the four of us alone.

"Too bad I'm not into men. He's easy on the eyes," Francis says, watching him walk away.

"Agreed," Luna adds with a laugh. "You've got good taste, Ms. Francis."

"In the meantime, why don't we do some research?" Francis claps her hands, moving away from the door. "I have a laptop in the other room. There has to be something on Kragen. He may not be human, but he has to have a weakness. Everyone has a weakness."

"Kragen doesn't have weaknesses," I retort.

"That's not true," Thorne argues. "He has one."

"Elsie," Francis fills in the blank. She turns toward me. "You're his weakness. The one that got away. The one he could never control."

"I'm not his weakness. I'm his obsession. The two are not synonymous."

"They're right," Luna agrees. "You're his weakness. You're the key to ending him."

a distant relative

WE SPEND the better part of the afternoon searching the "internets," as Francis calls it, for any information on Kragen. Just as I suspected, we find nothing new.

"I've spent hours, months, hell...years searching for information on him and to find a way to bring him down. I've found nothing. I'm not sure what you all expect to find in one afternoon." I sit back, running my hands through my already messy hair.

"A loophole? A mistake? Something that tells us where to find him?" Luna says next to me.

"He doesn't make mistakes. Besides, I have no idea how old he is. No matter the case, I doubt he's going to be using the World Wide Web to store secret information. The man captained a pirate ship, for God's sake."

"Were you on the ship the entire time you were with him?" Thorne asks.

"Most of the time, yes. There were several times throughout the years that he would take me to an island somewhere. I was blindfolded and covered in silver when transported." My words bring sadness to Thorne's eyes, and I instantly regret telling him so much.

"That's it," Francis says. "That's the key to stopping him. Find that island, and you'll find him."

"Unless Kragen has experienced a radical change of heart, he's not on the island. He's out, searching for me."

"You said he captained a pirate ship?" Francis asks, moving across the room.

"Aye," Thorne answers. "I spent years looking for the ship with no luck."

She pulls a large book from the shelf, bringing it to our small group. "I acquired this last year. It's the manifest load from Blackbeard's ship after they captured him."

"Blackbeard, Blackbeard?" Luna asks. "How did you get your hands on that?"

"A woman never tells her secrets." Francis smiles. "You know Blackbeard sailed around these waters at one time." She opens the book toward the back, flipping through several pages before settling on one in particular. "Here." She points. "Read this." She hands the book to her ancestor.

"I'm not sure what I'm supposed to see," he confesses.

"Here." She points again. "Mixed in with all the items he stole, it lists a stowaway."

"That's not unusual during that time," he argues.

Francis takes the book, turning to another page. "This lists a man who was found bound with silver and blindfolded in the bows of the ship." She turns another page, reading the description aloud.

"The man was wearing only a pair of trousers despite the weather being brisk. His skin was as white as death, and his eyes as dark as night. When the chains were removed, he thanked us in an unfamiliar accent before killing three men and escaping within seconds. Each man was drained of blood."

"He was a vampire," I say out loud.

"Aye, there's no other explanation."

"The description sounds like a very strong vampire," Luna adds. "Why would he be captive on Blackbeard's ship?"

Francis moves quickly to the bookshelf, pulling out a much smaller book, resembling Thorne's journal I found in his room. She opens it, searching for something specific. "This is a copy of Blackbeard's journal."

"Where did you find that?" Luna asks.

"Walmart. They sell copies for the tourists." She hands the copy to me. "During July of 1717, Blackbeard spent quite a bit of time around the Outer Banks of North Carolina. The journal doesn't list what he was doing while there, but maybe that's where he met up with Kragen and acquired the vampire."

"Maybe that's where he took you," Luna adds.

"Maybe," I whisper. "Why would Blackbeard have one of Kragen's men?"

I shrug. "Payment? A partnership? Anything's possible with Kragen. I don't believe there is a limit to what he would do to gain wealth."

"What do we do now?" I ask the crowd standing around me.

"We gather an army and go kick some ass." Luna raises her hands high in the air.

"Slow down, William Wallace. This journal was written three hundred years ago. Kragen's not dumb enough to still be hiding in the same location," Thorne adds.

"Why wouldn't he be?" Francis asks. "If no one has found him before now, why would he move? I wouldn't."

"Blackbeard found him."

"And he's dead," she adds.

"We can't do this alone," I answer finally.

"We don't have to." Luna pulls her phone from her pocket. "Micah texted a few minutes ago. His Alpha agreed to meet us tonight."

"How'd he get your number?" Francis asks.

Luna winks without answering. "He's asked us to meet in a bar on Broad Street at seven o'clock."

"That's in just a few hours," Francis says. "What does one wear to a meeting with the lycan Alpha?"

"Francis, I think it's safer for you to stay here. None of us knows what to expect when we get there," Thorne says.

"No offense, but *hell* no. I've lived seventy-four years being careful. This is the most exciting thing that's ever happened to me. I'm going."

I smile at her words. "I'll keep her safe," I reassure her grandfather.

We spend the next hour researching possible locations for Kragen to be hiding in the Outer Banks. We've narrowed it down to four different locations when Francis enters the room wearing a pair of blue jeans, cowboy boots, and a plaid shirt.

"Does this work?" she asks, doing a full turn in the middle of the sitting room.

Thorne whistles, bringing pink to her cheeks. "Looking good, Francis."

She smiles at his words. "Thanks, Grandpa."

"It's time to go," Luna announces. "We don't need to be late. It's a sign of disrespect in the lycan world."

"We can be there in ten minutes," Francis says. "It's an easy walk from here. I've been there many times. However, I never realized there were lycan there. Now it's much more interesting."

Right on time, the four of us approach the bar. To the unsuspecting eye, it's a normal bar. To the lycan of

Charleston, it's the home of their Alpha. "Ready?" I ask the group.

Luna opens the door, and we enter a nearly empty room. "Where is everyone?" Francis asks.

"It's early for the bar scene," Luna answers.

Micah appears out of nowhere. "This way." He turns, and we follow him to a door in the back of the room.

The man behind the desk is larger than anyone I've met before. He stands, towering over the rest of us. "Dad, these are the ones I told you about." Dad?

Luna bows her head toward the Alpha. "Luna Jamison. My Alpha, Christopher St. James, spoke highly of you and your pack."

"Christopher is a good man," the Alpha answers. He looks at the rest of us. "I'm Connor McFadden, and this is my son Micah, whom you've already met." He motions to several chairs in front of his desk. "Please." Thorne and I take the lead and sit down. "Tell me, what do two vampires, a lone lycanthrope, and a human need from my pack?"

"I feel like there's a punch line there somewhere," Francis says with a laugh. The Alpha doesn't respond.

"I was taken over three hundred years ago and turned into a vampire against my will. Ever since I escaped, my maker has tracked me relentlessly," I answer.

Conner sits back in his chair. "Please don't take this

the wrong way, but what does that have to do with me or my pack?"

"Because he will come looking for me. He will not stop until he finds me, and when he does, he will wreak havoc on Charleston."

The Alpha stares at me, without answering. "This seems like a situation that could be handled by other vampires. Why involve lycan?" Micah asks.

"Because I don't have anyone else," I answer truthfully. "I was held against my will for over a hundred years. I was abused and tortured in every way possible. I've been on the run from him for over two hundred years, and I don't want to live that life any longer."

"What are you asking from us?" Connor asks.

"Manpower," Luna answers. "There are four of us. I don't know how large your pack is, but from your size and power, I imagine there are plenty who would be willing to help."

"My pack is large, but there are not many who will be willing to help a vampire. I can't force them to come to her aid, simply because she doesn't know anyone else."

I close my eyes, willing tears not to fall. "I understand." I stand from the chair.

"No, hold up," Francis says, moving toward the large man. "I've lived in this city my entire life. Hell, I was born in the dining room of the same house I live in today." She pats Thorne on the back. "Imagine my surprise when I discovered that this handsome young man is not only a vampire, but he's my grandfather several times removed. The city I grew up in was built on the willingness to help others. You have an opportunity to bring your two groups together. An opportunity to help someone when they truly need it. Vampire or no vampire, she needs your help." She looks around the room. "Hell, what else do you have to do? Entertain drunk tourists?"

"What's your name?" Connor asks.

"Francis Hawthorne. This is my great-great-great-grandfather, Captain Hawthorne Rex."

"I appreciate your words, Ms. Hawthorne, but I cannot risk the lives of innocent lycan for an issue that isn't our concern."

"Dammit," Francis says, moving away from the desk. I follow her to the door when an old black-and-white photograph catches my eye.

"May I?" I ask, pointing at the picture.

"Of course," Connor answers.

Picking up the photo, I run my fingers over the face of the young woman staring back at me. Her eyes peer into my soul, reminding me of someone I knew long ago. "Who is this woman?"

"My grandmother several generations back. Her husband drew that picture right after they were married."

"She's beautiful." I continue running my hands over the picture. The wind is knocked out of me the moment I realize why she looks familiar. The large eyes and round face are identical to my younger sister Bonnie.

"Elsie? Are you okay?" Thorne moves to my side.

"Was her name Bonnie? Bonnie Abernathy?"

Connor stands, moving closer. "How did you know that?"

Pulling the picture to my chest, I can't control the tears that flow. "My name is Elsbeth Abernathy. Bonnie is...was my younger sister."

"Elsbeth?" Connor repeats my name. "You're Elsbeth Abernathy?"

"Aye," I whisper. "My sister wasn't a lycanthrope," I state the obvious.

"No. My grandfather fell in love with a human. He was the alpha and could love anyone he wanted."

I wipe a stray tear. "Bonnie married a lycanthrope?"

"She did," he answers.

"Was she...was she happy?"

"Very," Connor answers. "Our family history is full of stories of her life and the things she did for both the human and lycan culture of the city." My mind flashes to the tiny girl who insisted I carry her to the ship and always stayed by my side.

"She died well into her nineties," Connor continues. "Together, they had six healthy and happy children. Your sister was the perfect mate."

"Sweet Bonnie," I whisper, hugging the picture closer.

"Stories of your disappearance were passed down

through generations." Connor looks down with his words. "I'm sorry for what happened to you."

"You have a chance to help her, to help us," Thorne adds. "I was the captain of the ship that brought Bonnie and Elsie to Charleston. The Bonnie I knew was full of spunk and would've stopped at nothing to help her sister. She would've done anything she could to help Elsbeth escape."

Connor sighs, sitting back at his desk. "I agree." He closes his eyes. "How can we help you?"

A collective sigh resonates through the small room. "We have reason to believe that Kragen is still keeping his home base in the Outer Banks of North Carolina."

"That's not possible," Connor argues. "Every inch of those islands has been explored, most of it is uninhabit-able. If there were a vampire pirate and a horde of vampires living there, someone would know."

"Maybe they do?" Francis says. "Until earlier today, I thought my belief in vampires and werewolves was the silly imaginings of an old lady." She motions around the room. "None of you hide in caves or dark rooms. You live in plain sight. What if they do, too?"

"Are you suggesting we go to North Carolina and search for them?" Connor asks.

"We won't have to look for them. Kragen will be here, looking for me." I set the picture down, wiping a tear from my wet face.

"I'll worry about Charleston. You two," he points at Thorne and me, "should go to North Carolina."

"For what reason?" Luna interjects.

"If your theory is right, Kragen will not be there anyway. If he's been there for three hundred years or more, he will have ties to the community. Find a way to hit him where it hurts." He motions toward his son. "Take Micah with you. While you're gone, we'll prepare for his arrival here."

a trip to the outer banks

THORNE, Micah, and I are ready to leave for North Carolina less than an hour after leaving the bar. It took several conversations with Francis to convince her that she would be more help here, with Connor and Luna, preparing the lycan for Kragen's eventual arrival in Charleston. She's still not convinced but finally relents and agrees to stay.

The drive to the airport doesn't take long. The few items I shoved into my backpack are close to me as Micah drives.

"You own a plane?" Micah asks, for the third time.

"Aye. It belonged to my maker, but I have full access to it at any time."

As promised, we pull into the airport and head straight to the tarmac and the awaiting private jet. We board, and the doors are up less than ten minutes later.

"We are shooting for a landing in a municipal

airport. The powers that be have requested a landing in Raleigh Durham, but we're going to ignore their request," a voice says over the loudspeaker. "With that being said, we should be arriving within the hour."

We're barely in the sky before the plane begins to descend. "What's the plan?" Micah speaks for the first time since boarding.

"I've been studying maps since leaving. Other than driving the length of the islands and stopping to ask people along the way, I don't have one," Thorne answers. "I don't know what we're going to find or if we'll even find anything."

"If Kragen has been here for centuries, the humans who know something will be smart enough to keep quiet," I add.

"It's going to be a rough landing," the pilot says over the speaker. "We should be fine, but hold on."

"What the hell?" Micah asks, looking through a small window. "Is this the normal pilot?"

Thorne laughs. "Yeah. He's good. We'll be fine."

Micah checks his seatbelt several times before pushing back in his seat and closing his eyes. Thorne and I would survive a crash—Micah wouldn't. The plane touches down and stops like a well-choreographed dance. Micah's sigh is loud enough to bounce off the walls of the plane.

"Perfect," the pilot says over the speaker. "I will await your return...if they'll let me."

I make a mental note to meet our captain. He's badass.

The airport is everything you'd expect a small rural airport to be. Not much of anything. A single runway and a small building are the only things on the property. An older man runs from the building, straight toward us. "This isn't going to be good," Thorne mutters.

"What the hell are you doing?" the man yells. "You could've run off the end of the runway. We're not set up for a plane of that size."

The three of us share a look. "We won't be long," Micah answers. "Do you have Uber up here?"

"Uber? No. Hell, no. Get that plane off the runway."

"The pilot is inside," I point toward the empty jet.

"Dammit," the man answers, moving past us.

"Looks like an Uber is out of the question." Micah pulls out his phone, holding it high in the sky. "It also looks like phone service is out of the question."

Entering the small building, I'm surprised to see only one other person inside. A young woman behind a desk sits a little straighter as we enter. "Hello?" She smiles. "How can I help you?" Her words are slow and drawn out as she stares at the men on either side of me. Honestly, I don't blame her.

"We need transportation. Is there a service here anywhere? Maybe a taxi or an Uber?" I ask, drawing her attention to me.

"Honey, there ain't no Uber in these parts. We don't get many tourists out here."

"How do people leave the airport?" Micah asks.

"Well, they drive their car here and then take it home. The only people that fly in and out of here are agricultural pilots and a few scientists now and again."

Thorne leaves my side, moving to the edge of the woman's desk. He leans on the corner, crossing one long leg over the other. "I love your accent. Where are you from?"

Her cheeks turn red as he speaks. "Charlotte," she answers. "You really like my accent?"

"I do. It's very...charming." In a normal world, I would be jealous of his attempt to charm this woman. Today, I find it amusing.

"Why, thank you. I like yours, too. It reminds me of that TV show. You know, the one with the time-traveling woman and the hot red-headed man? Outlandish? No, Outlander. That's it, Outlander."

Thorne reaches down, picking up her nameplate off the desk. "Brittney? Such a lovely name for a lovely lady." He takes special attention to roll his r's, and I resist the urge to roll my eyes. Brittney, however, has fallen in love, and I'm enjoying the entertainment.

"You know what?" She pulls her watch in front of her face dramatically. "I'm off the clock in ten minutes. How about I drive y'all where you need to go?"

"Brittney, you'd do that?" Thorne turns toward us. "I guess Southern hospitality isn't just a myth."

"Aye," Micah answers, using the worst brogue I've heard.

Brittney stands from her desk. "Give me a few." She brushes Thorne's shoulder as she passes.

Several minutes pass before Brittney appears again. Her hair looks freshly combed, and bright red lipstick covers her lips. "I'm ready if y'all are."

"We're ready," Thorne answers. We follow the woman to a dirty white minivan parked in front.

"I hope you don't mind the mess." She pushes a button, and the doors slide open on the side. "Let me move these out of the way." She unhooks two car seats, throwing them in the back seat of the van. "My babies are with my ex tonight, so this is perfect."

Micah and I climb in the middle row, shoving half-eaten french fries and leftover chicken nuggets to the floor, while Thorne climbs into the front. "Thank you, Brittney. You're a lifesaver."

"You're welcome, sugar. Now, where can I take you?"

"We're looking for someone," I speak for the first time in a while. "He's a distant relative of mine. His name is Kragen, but I'm not sure if he goes by another name."

"Is that his first name or last?" she asks.

Thorne turns toward me with a questionable look on his face. "We've never heard any other name besides Kragen."

"Okay," she answers. "Where in the Banks does he live?"

"We don't know that either," Micah answers.

"We were just hoping to drive the length of the Banks and ask the locals if they've got information," Thorne adds.

Brittney turns toward the vampire in her front seat. "That's your plan?"

"Aye," he answers, turning on the charm.

"You're in luck." Brittney smiles as she speaks. "My family has been here since people first started coming here. I know just who to ask." She pulls out of the parking lot, throwing the three of us backward in our seats.

The drive along the Outer Banks is beautiful. The sun setting over the Atlantic is the perfect backdrop for a minivan ride. Brittney has resorted to sharing stories from the Outlander series she's watched, and Thorne is pretending to listen.

I'm not sure how long we've traveled before she turns off the main road onto one covered with sand and gravel. "We're here," she says in a singsong voice. She pulls the van to a stop in front of a home high on stilts. Bright headlights shine off the wooden facade. "Let me go in first."

We watch as the chipper woman climbs two flights of stairs and knocks on the front door. "This feels like the beginning of a horror movie," Micah says beside me.

Brittney disappears into the cabin as soon as the door opens. Several minutes pass before she reappears. She bounces down the stairs with a smile on her face. "Come on in," she says, opening the driver's side door.

The three of us follow her to the door of the cabin. "Now, I need to warn you. He can be a bit cantankerous at times." She opens the door wide. "Papaw? These are the people I was telling you about."

"Hello, sir." Thorne takes the lead. "Thank you for allowing us into your home."

An older man stands from a chair in the corner of the dark room. Deer heads, large fish, and other animals adorn the wooden paneled walls. "What do you want?" he asks.

"We're looking for information on someone who lived in the Banks many years ago," I answer.

"Why not use one of them fancy new computers they have now? I've heard tell you can find anythin' from pussy to flowers."

"Papaw," Brittney reprimands. "Behave."

"I am behavin'." He moves closer toward us. "Who ya' lookin' for?"

"A man named Kragen. He would be around my age with dark hair and eyes," Thorne answers.

"Kragen, you say?"

"Yes, sir."

"I don't recollect anyone named Kragen in the Banks. Now, there is a man with the last name Kraver that kind of fits your description." Bumps cover my skin at the mention of the name. That has to be him.

"Do you know where we could find him?" Micah asks.

The old man huffs a laugh. "Hell, he used to hang out at the Minnow Bucket years ago. I heard tell that he still comes around every now and again."

"The Minnow Bucket?" I ask.

"It's a bar not too far from here," Brittney fills in the blanks.

"Weird thing though," the man continues. "I thought I seen him not too long ago. Been near thirty years since I seent him last. If it were him, he ain't aged a damn day." He makes a strange face. "Must have some strong genes to produce a kid that looks that much like him."

"Can you take us to the bar?" Thorne asks.

Brittney shrugs. "Sure." She turns toward the old man. "Thank you, Papaw. I'll bring you some gumbo tomorrow."

"I'd like that," he answers, moving back to his chair in the corner. "Bring me some of that cornbread when you do. It reminds me of your Mamaw's."

Brittney kisses the man on the forehead before leading us out the front door and back to the awaiting van. "Ready to go to a bar?" she asks, winking at Thorne.

"Aye," he answers, returning the wink. "I've never been to an American bar. This should be fun."

"Well, the Minnow Bucket isn't usually classified as fun." We drive ten more miles up the narrow road before she turns into a dimly lit parking lot. In front of us is a building that looks like it's been through its fair share of hurricanes. An old neon sign flashes on and off, along with the image of a fish being thrown out of a bucket of water. "This is it."

The moment the van pulls to a stop, I feel the sensation of something otherworldly. Someone or something is here. Micah, Thorne, and I share a look, telling me they feel it too.

"Don't look like many people are here tonight." Brittney exits the van.

The sensation grows as we walk through the front door. Micah and Thorne crowd around me protectively. Neither one of them would stand a chance against Kragen if he's the energy we're feeling.

"Brittney! What are you doing here on a school night?" an older woman welcomes us.

"Bobby's got the kids tonight. I'm bringing my new friends to my favorite establishment."

"Howdy, folks. What can I get you to drink?" she asks.

"Nothing for me," Thorne answers.

"Water," Micah adds. I ignore the question, searching every square inch of the room for the source of the energy.

"Sure thing, baby." She returns minutes later with Micah's water. "What brings you folks out here? We don't get many out-of-towners in these parts. Most tourists stick to the big cities."

"We're looking for a man named Kragen or Kraver?"

"Kraver?" the woman repeats. "I think he's out of town." She turns toward a man in the corner. "Jimmy? Is Kraver out of town?"

"Who wants to know?" the man answers. He stands, and every hair on my body stands at attention. He's a vampire and the source of the energy.

Thorne and Micah sense him and turn at the same time. "We're doing some genealogy research, and his name kept coming up," I answer.

A deep laugh fills the small room. "You've got the wrong person. Kraver can't have kids." He continues to move closer. "I smell him on you." He glares in my direction. "His blood runs through your veins."

I need to escape this building, now. "Where is he?" I refuse to back down.

"That's for me to know and you to find out," he continues. "Maybe that will be sooner than you think."

Thorne steps in front of me. "This will not end well for you. My friend and I will rip you to shreds."

Jimmy sniffs the air toward Micah. "Lycan dogs don't scare me."

"I'm not trying to scare you," Micah answers. "You'll be dead before that emotion reaches the surface. Where is Kraver?"

Jimmy smiles, revealing razor-sharp teeth. "It's a

good thing I'm feeling kind tonight." He backs up, giving us space. "He ain't here."

"Tell him we will find him, and when we do, his days are numbered," Thorne warns.

"Did you steal that from a book or something?"

"Or something."

Out of nowhere, Brittney steps in the middle of the vampire-lycanthrope pissing match. She's either brave or stupid. I'm not sure which. "Well, that was fun. Did you find the answers you were looking for?"

"Aye, we did," Thorne answers.

"That's right. Run, pretty boy...back to your rich maker. I can smell him all over you," Jimmy continues.

"My maker is dead, as yours will be, too." Thorne turns, wrapping an arm through mine and pulling me toward the door. Micah follows closely behind. Each of them offering their protection.

"Bye!" Brittney says behind us. "I'll see y'all Friday night. Mama's gettin' wasted." The lights on the van flash, and the doors slide open. "What was that back there? Were you trying to get yourself killed?" Brittney waits until we're several miles away before speaking. "Jimmy's somewhat of a loose cannon. If he does know this friend of yours, I can guarantee they're up to no good."

"That's an understatement," Micah answers.

We drive the rest of the way to the airport in silence, and I'm grateful. My emotions are all over the place at the moment, and I'm not sure what I'll say if provoked.

"It's been a pleasure to meet y'all. I hope you'll come back again, and we can explore during the daytime. The Outer Banks are truly beautiful," Brittney says as she pulls in front of the airport.

"Thank you for your time." Thorne hands her a wad of rolled-up money. "You have been an outstanding tour guide and extremely helpful."

"Oh, I can't accept this," she argues, trying to hand the money back.

"I insist." He smiles, and even in the dark, I can see the redness return to her cheeks.

"If you insist. Anytime you folks need a tour guide, let me know. I'm more than willing to help you out." She hands Thorne a piece of paper with numbers scratched on it.

I'm surprised to find the jet still sitting in the middle of the runway. The man who we saw earlier is sitting at Brittney's desk, and the anger has left him. "Hello?" he greets us.

"Is everything okay?" Micah asks.

"Yeah. Your pilot paid enough money he can park that damn thing anywhere he wants." He leans back, propping his legs on the desk. "Anytime you folks need to come back, we're open."

We walk back to the jet and climb on board. "Welcome back!" the invisible pilot greets us. "I hope you had an eventful evening. We will be departing for a return to Charleston shortly."

The sound of jet engines roaring to life echoes through the hull, and just as promised, we are in the air and on our way home.

three centuries too late

MICAH'S asleep within minutes of the jet taking off. Thorne is sitting next to me, and I'm grateful for his comfort. Being around Jimmy brought up memories of Kragen I'd rather forget. In fact, I thought they were gone, but now, in the stillness of the jet, my mind keeps flashing to the horrors of my time with him.

"Are you okay?" Thorne whispers.

"Yes, no...I don't know." Long fingers wrap through mine, offering comfort. "Being around Jimmy and feeling his energy brought some old wounds to the surface. After I left, I vowed never to allow myself to feel that way again. For the first time in two hundred years, I did."

"I'm sorry, Elsie. For what it's worth, you were amazing back there."

"If I'm going to get away from Kragen forever, I'm going to have to be strong. I can't let him get to me."

Thorne pulls me close as the plane begins its descent. We're on the ground in Charleston less than an hour after leaving the Outer Banks. The drive back to Francis's house from the airport seems to take longer than the flight.

"How'd it go?" she asks the moment the front door opens. She and Luna are crocheting something that resembles a blanket.

"We didn't find Kragen, but we found one of his men," Micah answers for the team.

"What happened?" Luna asks.

"We met Jimmy in a bar that Kragen, now known as Kraver, visits frequently," I answer.

Francis abandons her blanket project and is at her laptop minutes later. "Kragen may not have pulled up anything, but Kraver might."

"Can I ask the obvious question?" Luna says, buried under pounds of yarn. "What would you have done if you would've run into Kragen? Waved at him and left quickly? From what you said, he's deadly, and walking into a bar that he frequents was dumb." She looks around the room. "Am I the only one thinking clearly?"

I sit on a chair, defeated. "I don't know what I would've done," I answer truthfully. "But I had to find out if he was there."

"Gunner Kraver. Born in 1965 in Raleigh, North Carolina, residence now shows a small town in the Outer Banks," Francis says from her laptop. "That has to be him."

Something inside of me snaps. I stand, turning toward my new friends. "I can't do this. I thought I was ready, but I'm not. Thank you all for trying, but I have to leave. I can't stay here and put you in danger any longer." Without turning around, I run through the front door and don't stop moving until I'm standing in front of the Atlantic Ocean. The same damn ocean that brought all of this on. The same ocean where both true love and Kragen found me.

"Leave me alone, you son of a bitch!" I scream at the empty sea in front of me. My life was stolen from me. A life with Thorne by my side. The life I imagined. Gone. All at the hands of a monster. I don't fight the tears that fall. All our little extravaganza to the Outer Banks did, was alert Jimmy that one of Kragen's creations is still alive. Why the hell did I let them talk me into something so stupid?

"I'm sorry, Elsie," a familiar voice says from behind. "The last thing I wanted to do was hurt you."

My eyes close at the sound of Thorne's voice. "I know. It's not your fault. I let myself believe that maybe there was a chance that I could escape. There's not."

"I love you," he starts.

I turn quickly. "This is something that love won't fix. He's going to hunt me down, now more than ever. All we did was piss him off even more. He's not going to stop until you, me, Francis, and whoever else dares to get in his way are dead. I was stupid to think this might work."

"There's a chance it will work," he argues.

"They can't survive on a chance."

"I'm not giving up on you. Not this time. I refuse to stay in the background any longer. Together, we will fight. The lycan are prepared to join us. We stand a chance against Kragen and his men." Thorne moves closer. "Hell, if I need to, I'll call on every vampire I've ever met to join us. We will defeat him, Elsie. I will not accept anything less than that."

I step forward, crashing my lips into Thorne's. The moment we make contact, a desire I've only read about surfaces. I want him. I want every part of him and refuse to wait any longer. The intensity of our connection is indescribable, and I can't get close enough.

Tearing the fabric of his shirt, I rip it from his body, leaving it in shreds behind him. Seconds later, my hands work their way to his belt and pants. It doesn't take long until he's standing in front of me naked. Evidence of his desire stares me in the face.

"Acushla." He sighs. "Are you sure about this?"

"More sure than I've ever been about anything." I step back, pulling the T-shirt and leggings I'm wearing off, making sure not to take my eyes off his.

"God, you're beautiful," Thorne sighs. "Can I touch you?"

Chill bumps cover my skin with his words. "Yes," I whisper. Thorne takes his time as his large hand covers my bare breasts. The moment his skin touches mine, I sigh loud enough to be embarrassing.

Thorne lowers to his knees, wrapping his arms around my waist and pulling me closer. He buries his head in my stomach, kissing every inch of my bare skin. Soft kisses work their way to my breast. His mouth covers one nipple, caressing it with his tongue, while his hand gently rubs the other. This is what helped me to survive. Imagining this moment with Thorne is what kept me alive.

This is what love is. This is what I've been dreaming of. Thorne is my future. Desire takes over my body with the intensity of his touch.

"I want you inside of me," I whisper.

"I'm okay with that." He pulls away, sitting on the sandy beach behind him.

I lower myself, straddling his hips with mine. His erection touches the softest part of me, bringing me to the brink of orgasm almost instantly. Lifting higher on my knees, I line him up with me and slowly lower myself onto him. The sensation nearly sends me over the edge. Thorne fills me completely as I slowly begin to move the length of him.

"I've dreamed about this moment." He sighs, covering my mouth with his own, his tongue matching the tempo of my movements.

He flips me over, hovering above me as he moves faster. Grabbing hold of his ass, I push him deeper until pleasure explodes through my body. Thorne follows seconds later, pushing deeper until there's no space separating the two of us.

Thorne raises on his knees, pulling me with him. "That was everything I imagined it would be," he says, working to catch his breath.

"Aye."

An energy I hoped to never feel again, hits me like a brick wall, interrupting the bliss of our connection. I freeze in place, staring into the distance, willing it to not be true. "Elsie?" Thorne asks. "What is it?"

"We have to go," I demand. Thorne doesn't question my words, and we dress in vampire speed.

My nose fills with the undeniable smell of sulfur. I grab Thorne's arm, pulling him away from the coastline and into downtown Charleston.

"Did I do something wrong?"

"Kragen's here." My mind is a collage of confusion as I look around the city, searching for an escape.

"Where?" Thorne looks through the crowds of unsuspecting humans, going on with their lives. "Are you sure?"

"I spent one hundred years being held captive by him. I know his energy and smell. There's no denying it. Kragen's here."

"Francis," he whispers. "I have to protect her."

"We can't risk going back to the house. If he doesn't already know about her, we'll be leading him straight to her."

Thorne runs a hand through his messy hair. "Dammit, I will not leave my granddaughter to die at the hands of that man. I refuse to lose anyone else to that bastard."

I close my eyes, understanding his pain. "Micah and Luna are there."

"Micah and Luna don't stand a chance against someone like Kragen." He turns toward the house. "I have to try, Elsie. What if it were Bonnie or Charles?"

He's right. I'd do anything to save them. "Go. I'll lead Kragen away from the city."

"No, I won't leave you. There has to be another way."

"You're going to have to make a choice." My words are harsh, but we're out of time.

"Dammit!" he screams to the sky.

"I can take care of myself," I reassure him. "Get them to the lycan bar. I'll come to you when I can." I fight the tears threatening to fall. "I love you, Thorne."

"I love you, too. This is not the end, Elsie."

I watch as he disappears, heading back to the home he built centuries ago. "I'm here, you insufferable asshole," I scream. "I know you can hear me, mother fucker."

The smell of sulfur fills my nose once more, telling me he's following. I move at vampire speed, leading him away from town and away from the people I have to protect. The irony of the situation isn't lost on me. I sacrificed my life to save my family once before. It seems history repeats itself.

Each time the smell recedes, I stop, waiting for him to follow, and each time, he does.

Our chase continues well into the night and through several states. While waiting for him to follow, I've checked my phone several times, and try not to focus on the reason why Thorne hasn't messaged me. Wiping the "what ifs" from my mind, I continue moving, pulling Kragen further away from Thorne and the people of Charleston.

I'm in the middle of a wheat field when I stop again, checking my phone and searching for Kragen's scent. There are still no messages from Thorne, and the smell of sulfur is further behind than before, which means I can rest for a few minutes.

Running uses my energy. On cue, my stomach growls loudly, letting me know I need to eat if I plan on keeping up this cat-and-mouse game.

Approaching the outskirts of a town, I stop, listening for a quick hit. Bars and the homeless are the easiest places to hunt. Preying on someone while they're in a weakened state is a cowardly move, but I'm fresh out of chivalry at the moment. I pick up on faint laughter and bad music not too far away, focusing on what sounds like a bar or nightclub still holding on to a few remaining patrons.

I follow the sound, ending at a small building on the side of a dead-end road. Motorcycles fill the parking lot, along with a few older model pickup trucks. A few people are stumbling toward their vehicles, clearly too inebriated to be driving.

Stepping inside, I find my victim quickly. A large man at the bar is yelling at the bartender, who has cut his alcohol off for the night.

The young female bartender seems unfazed by his tirade. "Go home, Gary. You're drunk."

"I want the beer I paid for, bitch," he yells.

I move to his side. "Gary, is it?"

He turns toward me. "What's it to you, whore?"

I look into his eyes. "I love a big, strong man. I have some beer in my truck. I'd love to share one with you." I rub his arm for effect.

Gary's angry face turns in a minute. He smiles, and his breath reaches my face before his words do. "See, I don't need your beer," he spews at the bartender. He turns back toward me. "Take me to your beer," he says as I lead him away from the building.

I move toward a truck in the back corner of the lot and pretend to have trouble opening the door. "What's the matter, little lady? Is that big, bad door too much for you?"

I laugh. "I guess so. Would you mind using those muscles of yours to open it for me?"

Gary smiles, moving in front of me. He pulls the handle, finding the door locked. The moment he turns back to me, I'm on top of him, pushing him against the metal. Within seconds, his heart rate slows as I drain him of nearly every last drop of blood. I pull away, leaving him alive, and watch as his body slowly slides down the side of the truck, his eyes fixed on mine.

"Thank you for your service, Gary," I whisper, wiping the blood from my mouth. "Be nicer to women."

I turn, ready to continue the game I've played with Kragen all night to see an image from my nightmares. Standing at the edge of the parking lot is the man I've been running from for two hundred years.

He's wearing a pair of khaki pants, a plaid button-up shirt, and a pair of loafers. His dark hair is tied behind his neck, making him look like a model, rather than the psychopathic killer he is.

"He's still alive," Kragen states the obvious. "Seems you're losing your edge." His words are no louder than a whisper as he speaks for my ears only.

"What do you want?"

He laughs deeply. "What do *I* want? I believe you know the answer to that question already. Don't bore me with menial conversation. It's beneath you."

"Fuck you."

"If you insist. However, I believe you need a shower to wash the stench of that captain off first. I smell him on and *in* you." He wrinkles his nose in disgust.

"How'd you find me?"

One side of his mouth lifts higher than the other. "I never lost you, my dear. I just let you run for a little bit. I do hope it was fun while it lasted."

"I won't go back."

"I don't remember offering you a choice."

"You're going to have to kill me," I retort.

In less than the blink of an eye, he's in front of me. "What would be the fun in that?" He runs a long finger along my cheek. "No, my dear. You're far too much fun to play with."

I jerk away, spitting in his eye. "I hate you."

"I have missed that tongue of yours, but flattery will get you nowhere." His hand wraps around my throat, and he pushes me against the truck door. "It's time to go now, Elsbeth Abernathy. It's time to go *home*."

"I'm not going anywhere with you."

"This feels strangely familiar, doesn't it?" Long arms wrap around my body, lifting me high into the sky.

an entire damn pirate ship

UNLIKE THE LAST time Kragen carried me away, this time I'm fully conscious. We're flying high in the sky in plain sight to anyone below. His arms are wrapped around me, and his body above mine, holding me tightly to his chest.

"Where are you taking me?" I scream.

"Home," he answers. "Where you belong."

"My home isn't with you."

His chest vibrates as he laughs at my words. "Your naivety is amusing." Kragen lands minutes later in front of a black SUV. A man I recognize from the Outer Banks exits with a smile plastered across his face.

"Hello, again," Jimmy says. He reeks of alcohol, blood, and insanity.

Mustering the largest amount of spit I can, I fling it in his face, hitting him directly in the mouth. Jimmy wipes the spit before backhanding me with the same hand. "Bitch," he mumbles.

Before I can respond, Kragen has the large man backed against the door of the SUV, with the hand that slapped me broken nearly in half. "Who gave you permission to do that?"

"She spit on me, man. Who knows where that whore's mouth has been."

Kragen turns into the monster that's haunted me for centuries. His face contorts into something from a horror movie. Sharp teeth become more pronounced as he transforms from the man he was earlier into the vampire I remember from years ago.

"Don't touch her again," he snarls. "Do I make myself clear?" Jimmy struggles against Kragen's strength. "I'm not asking twice."

"Yes," Jimmy answers.

"Good," Kragen backs away, straightening his wrinkled shirt. "Now, apologize."

Jimmy makes eye contact with both Kragen and me. "I'm...sorry." He stumbles through the words.

"Fuck you, Jimmy," I answer.

"That's my girl," Kragen says, patting my shoulder. He turns back to the injured vampire. "Take us home."

"Yes, sir," Jimmy responds, opening the driver's door. Kragen opens the back door, shoving me inside.

We sit in silence as Jimmy drives along the familiar roads of the Banks. The sun is beginning to rise, casting an eerie glow over the water.

Not too far from the Minnow Bucket, Jimmy turns down a secluded road. To the unsuspecting eye, it wouldn't even appear to be a road. The SUV bounces along potholes as he carefully maneuvers through the maze of trees.

"Where are we going?" I break the overwhelming silence of the drive.

"I already told you. Home."

The density of the trees clears, giving way to a large inlet, surrounded by old live oak trees. Sitting in the middle of the inlet is something I never thought I'd see again. Kragen's ship is anchored, looking every bit the same as I remember from two hundred years ago. Holy shit. There's a pirate ship in North Carolina.

"Is that your ship...the same ship?"

"It is," he answers. Pride shows through his voice. "She's beautiful, isn't she?"

"How?"

"Just takes a little upkeep."

Jimmy pulls the SUV to a stop, parking next to a small dinghy. Along the inlet, several men are walking around, performing their daily duties as if a pirate ship and a small horde of vampires is normal.

"Do these men realize they're not in the 1700s?"

Kragen laughs. "They're vampires. It doesn't matter what century they think they're in." He turns toward me. "Don't try anything stupid. I will not hesitate to kill you."

He pulls me from the back seat, making sure to keep

my hands bound behind my back. I can't take my eyes off the ship in front of me. How has he kept it hidden all this time? The sight sends chills down my spine.

Kragen shoves me toward the dinghy. "Get in." I follow directions as Jimmy grabs the oars. We work our way across the crystal blue water of the inlet to the side of the ship. I can't imagine how he managed to get it in here. The ship looks exactly like it did the day I escaped.

"Get up the ladder," Kragen demands. I ignore his demand and leap from the dinghy to the deck of the ship. He follows behind, landing beside me with a smile. "I see you've gained a little rebellion since you left."

He grabs my arms, pulling me toward the back of the ship and toward the room where I spent one hundred years locked inside. "Get in."

"No," I refuse. "I will not return to the bottom of the ship. You'll have to kill me first."

Kragen smiles, revealing the sharp teeth I remember. "Very well. Where would you like to go?"

"Home," I retort.

"Since that option is off the table, let's try again. Where would you like to go?"

I move to the edge of the deck, overlooking the water below, and sit. "Here's fine for now."

Watching the men move around on land and deck, my mind reels over possible outcomes from this scenario. Once Thorne realizes I'm not going to meet him at Connor's office, will he come looking for me?

Did he get there in time to save Francis and the lycan? Questions fly through my mind in rapid succession.

Kragen sits at a makeshift desk, not far from my chosen spot. The man working in front of me is different. Not only is he dressed in modern clothing, he's sitting behind a laptop, working. If I didn't know better, I'd think he was normal.

Other vampires are walking around the deck, working on different projects of their own. I recognize a few of them, but most are new faces. Some are dressed in modern clothes, while others are dressed the same as they were three hundred years ago. A young woman wearing a dress very similar to the one I wore all those years ago approaches me, standing several feet away. Her cheeks are sunken in, and her once vibrant eyes hold no light.

"Are you hungry?" she asks, rolling up her sleeve. Her arm is covered in scars. Anger fills me at the thought of these vampires using her as their donor. Our saliva heals wounds. The fact that her skin is covered in scars means that none of these assholes even bothers to heal their wounds for her.

"No. Thank you." I stare at the young human girl. "Do you need help?" I whisper.

Her eyes close, no doubt holding back tears. "No." She bows slightly. "Please let me know if you're hungry."

"What's your name?" I ask before she walks away.

"Maddie."

"How old are you, Maddie?"

"Twenty." Her voice shakes as she speaks.

"Are there others like you here?"

"Yes."

"Get away from her, wench," Kragen yells from the other side of the deck. Maddie bows slightly before scurrying below.

"You've resorted to kidnapping young girls for food?"

"Kidnapping is a strong word," he retorts. "She's more of a *volunteer*."

"How many *volunteers* do you have?"

He huffs a laugh. "Enough to feed my crew. I've turned over a new leaf. They're here because they want to be."

"I see you're still full of shit."

He sits back in his seat, staring at me. "You've grown quite brave in your time away, haven't you?"

"I didn't have a choice," I retort.

Kragen stands, moving in front of me. "You'll find a change of clothes in my quarters. Go wash that vampire's scent off. It repels me."

"Good. We're even."

"Don't confuse who you're talking to, my dear. I may have conformed to society on the outside, but I'm still the same man I was all those years ago." He steps backward, giving me space. "Clean his stench off of you —now."

I stand. The voice inside is screaming at the vampire

in front of me. Elsbeth from three hundred years ago would've cowered in his presence. Elsbeth of today wants to kill him. Rebelling at this stage is pointless. I don't stand a chance alone. Maybe Luna was right. With the help of the lycan, we could destroy him.

Looking around the ship at the few men on board, along with the few wandering around the inlet, I make a decision—one that will free me from Kragen forever, or one that will end in my death. Either way, I don't have a choice. Thorne will find me. He's proven that already. I have to stay alive long enough for them to get here. In the meantime, I will learn everything I can. No matter how well-prepared Kragen is, there has to be a weakness—a way to defeat the undefeatable.

I make eye contact with Kragen. "I apologize." I smile slightly as I speak. "I'll go clean up now."

He turns, giving me room to move around him. He doesn't respond, but I feel his eyes on my back as I move toward the captain's quarters.

When I was on the ship before, I was never allowed on deck or anywhere near his quarters. The opulence of the room is definitely not what I expected. The walls and floor are covered in deep mahogany. A large table takes up space in the middle of the room with enough chairs to seat his entire crew. A desk is in the far corner, along with a bookshelf beaming with leather-bound books of all colors and sizes. If I didn't know this belonged to Kragen, I would never believe it.

Hanging on a large wardrobe is a silk dress that

would've been the rage in fashion in 1700. Young Elsbeth would've been in heaven to wear such luxury. Vampire Elsbeth is trying to figure out how to move in such an atrocity.

Behind a large dressing screen is a modern bathtub, complete with running water. I turn the water on, filling the tub with steaming water. His ship may look the same, but he's added a few upgrades over the years.

I take my time, washing my hair several times and scrubbing my body until my skin turns pink. If I'm going to play the role of a submissive girl, I need to fully commit. I take a deep breath, willing the thoughts of Thorne and our time together away from my mind. In the years I've been a vampire, I never had anyone I could depend on. No one was coming to rescue me. My survival was purely because of me. I close my eyes with the realization that Thorne will come, and with him, a small army of lycan. I have to dare to hope there will be an end to this nightmare I've lived for three hundred years.

Staying in the tub until the water turns cold, I find a fluffy towel in the wardrobe, along with the items needed to keep my hair from looking like a frizzy mess. I take my time, putting extra care into my appearance. Pulling my dark hair into a thick braid, I stare at the woman in the mirror. Bright green eyes stare back, offering their support. I'm not the shell of a woman that Kragen once held. I will take him down or die trying.

The dress is difficult to get into without help, but I manage. It's a perfect fit, hugging my curves in all the right places. Did he have it made for me?

A soft knock sounds on the door. "Who is it?"

"Your captain," Kragen's voice sounds through the wood. "I was being polite to knock. Open the door."

I follow orders, stepping away from the door and giving him space to enter. Kragen stops in the doorframe, staring at me.

"That's better." He nods approvingly at my appearance. He sniffs the air in front of me. "You smell better, as well."

"Thank you for the dress." Trying to be charming to the man that I've held nothing but hatred for is proving more difficult than I expected. Every fiber of my being is fighting against me.

"You look lovely. Dinner will be delivered any minute." He motions to the table in the middle of the room. "Please, have a seat."

My stomach drops at his words. Without arguing, I move to a seat at the opposite end of the large table. Kragen chooses the seat next to mine. The door opens as Jimmy enters, dragging the young woman I met earlier behind him. "This one is ready," he says with a smile.

"Lovely," Kragen answers.

"Maddie?" I say her name without thinking.

"Hi," she whispers, wiping tears from her cheeks.

Jimmy brings her to the table, slamming her head into the wooden surface. I stand, moving toward her.

"Sit down," Kragen demands.

"She's hurt," I argue.

"So? Sit down." I close my eyes and lower back to the seat. Following his orders takes everything I have. "Drink from her."

"I'm not hungry."

"Drink from her," he repeats.

"No."

Kragen stands, grabs Maddie by the wrist, and drags her closer to my seat. "Drink, or I will."

I know without asking, he will take every drop of blood left in her weak body. I make eye contact with the young girl, offering apologies through my gaze. Licking her arm to numb her skin, I bite into her arm and drink. Her blood is weak and tastes of other substances. Maddie's eyes close as I pull away, making sure to leave her more than enough for another day.

"Good girl," Kragen whispers in my ear. "Now, kill her." Maddie's eyes open as new tears form.

Jimmy's laugh fills the room as the blood I took bubbles in my stomach. Without planning or thinking, I move behind Jimmy, biting into his neck and ripping his head from his body before he has time to recognize my movement.

Kragen stares at the spectacle in front of him with a sickening smile covering his face. I move protectively in front of the young girl who's crying uncontrollably.

"Well done, my dear," Kragen says with a soft clap. "Well done."

Pulling Maddie with me, I back out of the door onto the deck of the ship. My dress is covered with blood, which strangely makes me sad.

"Go," I tell the scared woman. "Get out of here."

"There's nowhere to go," she cries. "I don't even know where I am."

"Hide in the trees." I nod toward the mass of greenery surrounding us. "Go, now." She nods before running off the deck and jumping into the water below. I turn, expecting Kragen to be behind, and find the deck empty. What the hell?

For a moment, I consider following her. I could swim faster than he could follow and get both of us out of here, but escaping would only prolong the chase. Kragen's proven that. Instead, I sigh and attempt to wipe the blood from the front of my skirt before moving back toward his quarters.

Opening the door, I find him in the same spot as before. He's leaning back in his chair, nursing a glass of red liquid, with his legs crossed at the knees. "Back so soon?" he asks.

"I hope that one wasn't your favorite." I nod toward the body on the floor.

Kragen crinkles his nose. "I only have one favorite." He toasts the air in front of him in my direction. "Besides, I haven't had a show like that in quite a while.

You have proven to be very entertaining. Well worth my investment."

I move back to my earlier seat, sitting across from my captor. "Why me, Kragen? During my time on this ship, you brought many captives on board and disposed of them quickly. Why keep me? Why turn me? Why torture me? Why not kill me and put me out of my misery?"

"You intrigue me," he answers, taking a sip of his liquid. He nods toward Jimmy's body. "Clearly, the entertainment aspect alone is worth the time spent."

"I'm not your captive any longer."

"No, you're to be my wife."

fast food

I STARE ACROSS THE TABLE, not sure I heard Kragen correctly. "Your wife?" I echo, trying not to laugh.

"Congratulations. It's an honor many have sought." He takes another drink before standing from the table. "The ceremony will take place this afternoon." He stands to leave the room.

"No."

Kragen turns back with a genuinely puzzled look on his face. "No?"

I need to stall whatever is going on here long enough for Thorne to arrive. Dear God, let him arrive. I clear my throat before speaking. "I mean I will need more time to prepare. There's a dress, and...and decorations, and..."

He studies my face for a few minutes before speaking. "Friday then." He turns, leaving me alone in his quarters.

Shit. What is today? I stumble through my brain, finally deciding that today is Tuesday. That leaves four days for Thorne to find me. Will that be enough time? Will he find me? Is he even searching? I flush the intrusive thoughts from my mind and focus on how to stall the wedding as long as possible.

I spend the next few hours staring at the door, waiting for the next "guard" to be sent into the quarters. Surprisingly, I've been alone since Kragen left. Several more hours pass before I gain the nerve to see if he locked me inside.

Slowly turning the knob, I'm shocked when the door opens. I step outside, expecting to find several guards, and am surprised to find the deck empty. What the hell? I spent a hundred years locked in silver chains —now he gives me free rein of his ship?

I move toward the railing, overlooking the crystal blue water. Searching the banks of the inlet, I look for the young girl who escaped earlier, not finding any evidence that she's alive...or dead.

In order for Thorne to stand any chance against Kragen's men, I need to find every detail I can about this place. Taking my time, I count each of the men on land, noticing any distinguishable markings about them. I spend the better part of the afternoon putting them to memory.

Three of Kragen's men look familiar, while the other

five I don't recognize. Most of the men seem to be on autopilot. Their behavior isn't like anything I've seen before. If I didn't know better, I'd think they were mindless drones instead of lethal vampires.

"Are you hungry, miss?" a young voice says from behind.

I turn, finding a boy, no older than fifteen or sixteen, standing alone on the deck. The clothes he's wearing are nothing more than rags, with more holes than fabric. His mousy blonde hair is covered in dirt and blood, and his eyes are full of sadness.

"What's your name?" I ask.

"David," he answers. His voice is shaky as he speaks.

"It's nice to meet you, David. My name is Elsie. How old are you?"

"Eighteen," he lies.

"Are you okay, David?"

He closes his eyes before speaking. "Yes, ma'am. Are you hungry?"

I move closer to the boy. "No. Thank you for offering." He turns to leave. "David?"

"Yes, ma'am?"

"How many of you are there on this ship?"

"Five."

"Will you take me to the others?" David's eyes open wide with fear. I move closer still, locking my eyes with his. "I won't harm them. I am here to help you. You can trust me."

His pupils dilate with my compulsion. "Follow me," he whispers.

He leads me off the main deck into the familiar hallway that leads to the room I lived in for many years. The closer we get, the stronger the odor of death becomes. We enter, and I resist the urge to cover my nose.

The four people in front of me are nothing more than children. Their bodies are covered in wounds, and most are barely conscious.

"Oh, my God," I whisper. "How can I help you?"

"We're here to serve you," a young girl says, sliding herself backward against the hull. "Are you hungry, miss?" Her voice weaker than moments before.

"Can you walk?" I ask.

She struggles to stand, finally making it with the help of David. "Yes, ma'am," she answers.

"Take her to the captain's quarters," I demand. "I'll bring the others."

David's eyes take on a look of fear I'd recognize anywhere. "Maddie was the only one allowed in his quarters, and she disappeared."

"It's all right," I reassure him. "I'm not going to let anything happen to you."

I watch as the duo slowly makes their way out of the room toward the quarters, while I gather the other three up and follow behind. I don't care what Kragen says, I will not allow anyone else to suffer as I did.

I move in front of David, opening the door for them.

"Are you sure it's all right, miss? The captain is going to be angry."

"I don't care if he is. I will not allow him to harm you." I know that's a promise I can't keep if it comes down to it, but I will die trying. I set the three unconscious girls down carefully and watch as David does the same.

"There's water in there." I point at the bathtub. Get them something to drink, and I'll find food.

"We usually eat rats," David says, following my directions. His words bring back memories of my life in the same room. A life where rats kept me alive after the transformation.

"Aye, I remember," I answer, wishing the ghosts of memories away.

On a ship full of vampires, there is no food anywhere to be found. If I leave to search the inlet and Kragen discovers what I've done, I have no doubt he won't hesitate to kill every one of them.

"Thank you, ma'am," David says, bringing water to the weak group of humans.

"Don't thank me yet. We haven't gotten you out of here yet."

The smell of sulfur hits me before the sensation of Kragen approaching does. Shit. "Get under the table, now," I whisper.

"Ma'am?" David looks confused.

"Hide, now!" I demand.

David drags one of the unconscious girls under the

large table, and I follow behind with the others. Just as I stand, the door to the quarters opens, revealing the source of my nightmares.

"Hello, my dear." I cross my arms in front of my chest without responding. He lifts his nose into the air, sniffing the unmistakable smell of death, and smiles with recognition. "You wouldn't happen to know what happened to the crew's dinner, would you?"

The sound of whimpering whispers from the hiding place. "It seems they've disappeared," he continues, stalking closer toward the table. "I wonder where they are?" He bends down, closer to the humans. "Come out, come out, wherever you are."

"Stop!" I demand. Moving vampire speed, I stand between him and the terrified children. "They are nothing more than babies. You can't force them to be here."

Kragen stands. "Force? Who said anything about forcing? Did I force anyone?" he asks the group hiding.

The whimpers intensify. "See," he continues. "No one said anything about being forced. They're free to go anytime they wish."

"Then they choose to leave now," I interrupt.

"I'm afraid I can't allow that, Elsbeth."

In a moment of either complete grandeur or stupidity, I'm not sure which, I stand my ground. "If you want my hand in marriage, you will free them."

Kragen stands, staring at me. I can't tell from the look on his face what's about to happen. I refuse to let him see how terrified I am. I mask my energy the best I can, hoping to hide the terror I feel inside. "Are you refusing your hand in marriage if I don't allow them to go?"

"Aye," I answer.

He moves toward the door, opening it wide. "Very well, you may go."

I stare at the creature in front of me. "Nothing will happen to them?"

He shakes his head. "Nothing will happen to them."

"I have your word that they'll leave the ship without harm?"

"You seem so untrusting of me, my dear." His words send chills down my spine.

"It's okay," I whisper to the group. David is the first one out. The look on his face mirrors my own.

"Welcome, child." Kragen moves away from the door, giving him space. The girls who were unconscious earlier have awoken and are crawling behind him. I rush to their sides, offering help.

The small group works its way to the railing of the ship. "How are they going to get down?" I ask, looking over the water.

"There's a ladder," Kragen answers, pointing at the flimsy rope ladder attached to the side of the ship.

"They're too weak. They'll never make it."

Kragen shrugs. "That is not my concern."

"You promised," I argue.

"No, my dear. I gave my word they would leave the

ship without harm. What happens on the way down wasn't part of the deal."

"Semantics."

He raises his eyebrows. "Quite possibly."

I wrap the three weakest girls in my arms and jump from the main deck to the inlet, bypassing the water altogether.

"How did you do that?" a weak voice says as I lay them on the sand.

"Rest. I'll be back." I jump back to the ship, landing in front of David and the girl who walked into the quarters.

"You impress me, my dear," Kragen says from the deck.

I ignore his words, picking up the two remaining humans and copying my movements from before, I jump them close to the others. "What do we do now?" David asks, looking into the seemingly endless forest.

"You live." The SUV that brought me here is sitting in the same spot as before. Climbing inside, I'm grateful for Jimmy's stupidity and the keys still being in the ignition. I hand them to David. "Get them out of here."

"Wait!" a voice yells across the inlet. "Don't leave me here!" I turn, finding Maddie, working her way across the dense forest toward us. Behind her lurks something from nightmares. Kragen. His humanness has transformed into the creature from my memories.

"No!" I scream seconds before Kragen bites into her neck, draining the remaining blood from her weak body. I watch in horror as her lifeless body falls to the ground in silence.

"Did he just…" David begins.

"He did. Go, now!"

"I don't know how to drive," he answers.

"At this point, it doesn't matter. Just put it in drive and floor it. I'll keep him here." The SUV roars to life as he slides the seat as close to the wheel as possible. "Don't stop until you get to a police station!" I yell as he slides the gear shift, and the wheels spin.

Kragen is in front of me in an instant as the SUV pulls away from the edge of the water. "Leave them alone," I warn.

He smiles as the SUV continues to bump over the terrain, working its way toward an escape. "I will say, I'm enjoying this feisty side of you. It's cute."

Cute? What the hell?

"Fuck you, Kragen."

"Oh, you will, my dear. You will."

"You killed her," I nod toward the body of the young girl.

"Hmm?" he turns, following my line of sight. "Oh, her. She wasn't part of our deal."

"You are a son of a bitch."

Kragen shrugs, holding his arm toward me. "Shall we?"

"I'll never marry you," I retort.

"Then you won't be holding up your end of the

deal." He nods toward the path the SUV took. "Shall I stop them?"

"You wouldn't."

He's in front of me in a second. "Don't presume to know me, Elsbeth. You are nothing more to me than a monetary exchange to heighten my wealth." Hot breath touches my face. "I will not hesitate to end your life once you are no longer needed." Kragen wraps my arm through his, and together, we walk into the water toward his awaiting ship.

Vampires don't need to breathe, but the sensation of being underwater brings back terrifying images of my baths while a prisoner. As we approach the vessel, I notice two large anchors embedded in the sea floor. Both show signs of wear and deterioration.

Kragen grabs my arm and leaps to the deck of the ship. "Change your dress," he demands before turning and leaving me alone.

stranger from the past

I STARE at the closed door, not sure what just happened. What did Kragen mean by me being a monetary exchange?

Miraculously, a dress similar to the one I'm wearing is hanging on the side of the wardrobe. Water drips from every orifice of my body as I replay our conversation word for word, hoping for a clue into his insanity.

I dry off, using the towel from earlier, and change into the dry clothing. Copying my braid from earlier, I pile it on top of my head, the same way my mother would all that time ago.

Jimmy's body, or what's left of it, is still lying in the middle of the quarters. His eyes have glazed over, turning him into a character from a nightmare. "Bastard," I whisper, kicking his head across the room. It hits the mahogany wall with a sickening thud, leaving a dark stain behind.

A soft vibration echoes through the wooden room. It takes a few minutes to realize that the sound is coming from Jimmy's body. Oh, my God. A cell phone?

I search, finding the ancient flip phone in the front pocket of his jeans. "Dammit!" I stand, realizing the phone doesn't have access to the internet, meaning I don't have any phone numbers for the people I need to contact.

The phone vibrates again. The contact pulls up as "Britt-Britt."

"Hello?" I answer.

I'm met with silence on the other end. "Who the hell is this?" the voice finally speaks.

"Elsbeth," I answer. "Who is this?"

"Elsbeth, who?"

I sigh, not sure what to say. "Do you know Jimmy?"

"Yes," she answers. "I called his phone, didn't I? I'm his damn girlfriend. Or a friend with benefits, or...hell, I don't know what I am. Where is he?"

Looking at the body below me. "He...he let me borrow his phone. I've been kidnapped."

"What?"

"I've been kidnapped. Jimmy found me, but he's hurt, and I have his phone."

"Oh, my God. Where is he?"

"I don't know where we are." I soften my voice, hoping to sound like the scared woman I should be. "We need help."

"Elsbeth?" the woman asks. "Are you the same Elsbeth that I drove around the Banks the other day?"

"Brittney?"

"It's me, girl. Oh!" She goes quiet for a minute, and the sound of papers shuffling echoes through the phone. "That man you were with called looking for you earlier."

"Thorne? What did you tell him?"

"The truth. I ain't seen hide nor hair of you. He left his number."

"Call him! Tell him I'm not far from the bar and with Kragen." Brittney's quiet on the other end. "Brittney?"

"I'm here, just writin' it down. Tell Jimmy I'm coming."

"No, Brittney. You can't come here."

She sighs deeply. "We'll see about that." She hangs up the phone, and for the first time, I have a bit of hope.

Picking up Jimmy's body, I drag it outside, laying it in the sun. With the few vampires that I've seen die over the years, their bodies will usually disappear quickly. I'm not sure why Jimmy is still here. I place his head next to the body, stopping myself from kicking it off the side.

Looking around the room, I search for anything that will help me in a fight. I can hold my own, but against eight other vampires and my maker, I don't stand a chance. Shit! Where's a silver chain when you need it?

The door to the quarters opens without warning,

and Kragen bursts through. He's dressed in what has become the traditional pirate costume of modern times. Fringed pants, a puffy shirt, and a long sword complete his outfit. "Good, you're dressed, my love. We have company."

Two men enter behind him. Both are vampires and dressed in the finest fashions from the height of piracy. Where Kragen looks like a dollar store version, these men are fashionable and gorgeous.

"She's just as lovely as you said," the taller of them announces as they enter. "She'll do splendidly." His thick French accent makes it difficult to understand his words.

Do for what? Instead of asking, I smile, not sure what's expected of me. "Hello, gentlemen." I curtsy.

"Where's the treasure?" the shorter of the two asks. His accent isn't as pronounced as the first.

Kragen smiles. "All in due time, gentlemen. All in due time." He motions toward two open chairs at the table. "Please, sit down, and we will discuss the games."

The games? What the hell is he talking about?

"Excuse us, my dear. We need to talk in privacy," Kragen smiles a fake smile toward me.

"She stays," the taller man interjects. "It's rare to see a woman so well dressed in today's society."

"Very well," Kragen answers with a smile, pulling out a chair for me. I sit, facing the two strangers.

He clears his throat before continuing. "The games

are scheduled for tomorrow. The treasure has been safely secured. As per our agreement, your full payment is required before the games begin."

The French vampires share a look. "Half before and half after," the taller one answers.

Kragen closes his eyes, clearly frustrated with the negotiations. "Very well."

"Gentlemen," I interrupt, using my best Southern drawl. "Please forgive my ignorance of your being here." I smile, turning toward Kragen. "See, my fiancé doesn't always share the prizes for these games he does. My female brain is curious about yours." I resist the urge to pat myself on the back for my award-winning performance.

The shorter man smiles, matching my energy. "Mademoiselle, you are quite delectable."

"Why, thank you," I continue, turning on the charm.

"Keeping information away from such a lovely lady should be a crime," the man continues. He smiles and covers his mouth with his hand. "Our treasure is worth more than gold," he whispers with a sickening smile. "Twenty human feeders are on their way to us. We've paid for the deluxe edition of the treasure hunt." He claps his hands in excitement.

I focus on keeping my face from showing the turmoil inside. "Twenty humans?"

"Oui," he answers. "Kragen has promised the best crop, all under the age of sixteen."

My stomach drops. Twenty children to feed to vampires?

"Isn't that lovely?" he asks me.

"It is amazin'," I answer, hoping he can't read the turmoil I feel inside. "Where did you find these children?" I ask Kragen.

He smiles. "Oh, you know. Here and there."

The two vampires stand, signaling us to stand with them. "We will see you tomorrow."

"Good evening, gentlemen," Kragen answers.

The shorter vampire moves in front of me in an instant. Taking my hand into his, he licks the back of my hand before placing his lips gently on top. "Good evening, mademoiselle. Until we meet again."

Kragen wraps my arm through his, pulling me onto the deck of the ship behind the French vampires. The men jump from the deck to the sandy shore of the inlet before loading a large SUV similar to the one David escaped in hours earlier.

He keeps my arm held tightly in his until the lights of their vehicle disappear from sight. "Whatever you think you can do to stop this exchange is futile," he warns.

"How much are they paying you?"

"That is none of your concern. Neither is the treasure." He turns, walking away from me.

"Where are they?" My words are no louder than a whisper, but Kragen turns, facing me. "Where are you holding twenty children?"

"It doesn't matter," he answers.

"You're a monster."

"So I've been told."

"I won't allow you to do this," I continue.

"You're in no position to allow me to do anything." He disappears below deck. He's right. I have no power over anything Kragen does.

I pull Jimmy's cell phone out of my skirt, finding ten missed calls from Brittney's number. I text her, praying that it gets to Thorne.

> Kragen's ship is anchored in an inlet in
> the Outer Banks.

Being a flip phone, it takes longer than it should to text one sentence. The moment I hit send, the phone goes dark. "Shit!" I scream into the empty land. Did my message go through?

I resist the urge to throw the phone further than human eyes can track, instead, sliding it back into my skirt.

Twenty human children. My mind flashes back to boarding a ship very similar to this one with eight of my brothers and sisters, heading for what we hoped was a better life.

These twenty children belong to someone. Someone who is looking for them. I can't allow these "games" to take place. They deserve a chance to live. I don't know how, but I will stop this.

I spend the next few hours searching the ship for

any clues to where Kragen might be holding the "treasure," finding nothing.

I've felt helpless throughout my life, especially during my time on this ship, but knowing there may be nothing I can do to stop this charade is one of the hardest things I've ever done.

Back in Kragen's quarters, I'm glad he's given me the time alone. I don't want anything to do with him at the moment. My acting skills are gone. An energy I don't recognize moves closer to my location, bringing me to my feet. Something about it feels familiar, yet not at the same time.

I move toward the door, ready for whatever is about to enter. A soft knock brings chill bumps to the surface. "Elsie," a voice says from the other side. I refuse to answer. "Elsie," the voice repeats. "It's me. It's Bertram."

My heart stops at the mention of my brother's name. Is this a trick? Bertram can't be alive unless he's... he's a vampire.

"Bertram?" I whisper through the closed door.

"Aye," the voice answers.

"Prove it."

A deep laugh echoes in my ears. "Daddy used to call you Bethie. He was the only one you allowed to call you that. It was his special name for you."

I open the door, not sure what's going to be on the other side. A man has replaced the boy I remember. "Bert?"

"Aye, it's me," he answers. I don't hesitate. I move in front of him, wrapping my arms around his neck. He's at least a foot taller than me with a head full of dark hair.

"How is it possible?" I wipe tears as I speak. He flashes his teeth, showing two fangs. The same fangs I have. "I'm a vampire."

"Kragen?" I ask, knowing the answer.

"Aye." He looks down. "I was looking for you and got too close. Kragen found *me* instead and turned me into this." He runs his hands down his body. "Forced to work for him for all eternity."

"He can't keep you here," I argue. "You're free."

He huffs a laugh. "In a way, I am free. The sugar sickness made me weak, made me sickly. Now, I'm strong."

I wrap my arms around him a second time, relishing the fact that I'm hugging my younger brother. "I've missed you."

"Aye, I've missed you, too. I was told you were dead."

"Kragen would like me dead, I'm sure. I escaped."

His eyes grow wide with my words. "Then why are you here?"

"It's a long story." I move to the table, pulling a chair out for him. "Does he know you're in here?

"No, he left a while ago."

I spend the next few minutes filling my baby brother in on everything that's happened with Thorne, the Outer Banks, ending up back here, and the treasure hunt that's taking place tomorrow. He stares at me like a child during story time, hanging on every detail.

"Captain Hawthorne Rex is a vampire?"

I smile at his excitement. "Aye. He did it to find me. Is that the only part you were listening to?"

"No, I heard everything, but that grabbed my attention. Damn. I can't believe he did that." He slides further into his seat. "And he's gathering an army of werewolves to rescue you?"

"They prefer to be called lycan," I echo Luna's words. "Truthfully, I don't know if anyone is coming, and I refuse to allow these children to die. I don't know how to do this alone."

"You're not alone," he answers with a smile.

wedding of a lifetime

STARING AT MY YOUNGER BROTHER, I'm in awe of how much he reminds me of our father. He shares the same dark hair and bright blue eyes. The angles of his jawline form into a sharp point at his chin, bringing flashes of the last time I saw our father alive.

"Have you been on this ship the entire time?" I ask, hoping to clear the thoughts from my mind.

"No. After I was turned, Kragen left me alone on an island in the Atlantic."

"He left you? How did you eat?"

"Animal blood, mostly. Rats, mice…anything warm." He looks off at a distant memory. "I don't know how long I was there before he returned. When he found me still alive, he said I'd earned a place with his crew."

"I'm so sorry, Bert."

He shrugs. "Yeah, me, too. It wasn't all bad. It taught me how to survive."

The air between us becomes awkward. "Do you want to get away from Kragen?"

He slides back into his chair. "For the longest time, I did. Now, I don't know." He looks up. "Until I saw you, I didn't have a reason to leave."

I slide my hand on top of his. "We have each other."

"Aye, we do." Large fingers squeeze into mine.

"We have to stop Kragen and the games. As long as he's alive, he will continue finding ways to destroy lives."

Bertram stares at me in silence. His eyes close, and he takes a deep breath. "I know where the treasure is."

"The humans? Where?"

"A small warehouse not far from here."

I stand, pulling him with me. "Let's go. We have to save them."

"Slow down, Elsie. They're being guarded and bled by vampires around the clock. We can't just walk in there and free them. We're not prepared for that."

"There's no time to waste." The sun peeks over the horizon with my words. "Today is the day they're being sold."

"Elsie, sit down." Bert pulls me back to the chair. "The men who are purchasing the treasure aren't taking them for food." He closes his eyes and sighs. "Kragen calls it a game for a reason."

"What aren't you telling me?"

"The humans will be brought here to the inlet and set free."

Oh, my God. The realization of what Kragen's games are hits me. "The vampires hunt them for sport?" I fill in the blanks.

"Aye."

"Shit."

"Aye," he agrees. "It's nostalgic for the older vampires, and they pay quite well for the experience."

"How do we stop them?"

Bert runs a hand through his messy hair. "There are others who believe like I do."

"Will they help?"

"Truthfully, I don't know."

"They have to." I stand, moving toward a window. "How many?"

"It's not like we hold weekly meetings." He scratches his head again. "Three maybe."

"Are they strong?"

"Aye."

"We have to get to that warehouse and save the kids before they bring them here."

"No," Bert interrupts. "We don't stand a chance at the warehouse. We have to wait until they come here."

"If the humans come here, they'll die."

"Kragen is an arse, but he's an egotistical arse. He starts the games with a showcase of his strength. It's how he makes himself feel powerful."

"How many games have there been?" Horror fills

me, thinking of how many humans have died for his enjoyment and money.

"More than I'd care to remember." Bert closes his eyes at the memory. "He will sacrifice one of the humans as a show of strength before the games begin. It's his way of showing the hunters that he's the one in charge. During that time, the rest of the humans will be freed for the hunt."

"Can we gather the rest and get them to safety?"

"A few maybe, but not all."

"Dammit, Bert. I refuse to accept that answer." Anger fills me.

"Aye, I agree, but it's all I can give you at the moment. If I can convince the others to fight, between the five of us, we might be able to save half of them."

My sigh fills the wooden room. "Half is better than none. It's our only option."

Bert's face tells me he feels Kragen's energy the same time I do. "He's coming," I whisper.

"Aye." He stands. "The games are at sunset. I'll talk to the others but can't guarantee they're going to be willing to help." He wraps long arms around me, pulling me close. "I love you, Elsie."

"I love you, too." I watch as Bert silently leaves Kragen's quarters. As screwed up as it is to know that Bertram's a vampire, the fact that he's still on Earth gives me hope.

I hear what sounds like a car, followed by a familiar voice. "Elsbeth!" a woman yells.

Shit. I know without looking that Brittney is the voice I hear. How the hell did she find me?

"Elsbeth," she repeats. "Is that a damn pirate ship? Elsbeth!"

Opening the door, I run into the source of the sulfur smell. Kragen is standing on the other side with an amused look plastered across his face. "Hello, darling. It seems you have company."

"Leave her alone," I warn. "She has young children and has no idea what we are."

"I wouldn't dare harm a mother." The smile that covers his face doesn't mirror his words. "Let's go talk to her, shall we?"

We move to the edge of the deck, facing the minivan I remember from our tour. "Elsbeth, is that you? Are you okay, honey?"

"Brittney. I'm fine. You need to leave. Now."

"Who is that with you?"

I turn toward my captor. "Kragen is an old friend. You need to leave," I repeat.

The sound of a cracking branch draws her attention behind her. "Call them off," I warn Kragen.

"I don't see anyone." His voice sounds bored. "I cannot guarantee her safety."

"Are you sure you're okay?" Brittney continues. She's looking at the woods surrounding her as she speaks. I can smell her fear from here.

"Yes, I'm great. Better than ever."

I catch a glimpse of movement behind her, and my heart stops.

"Call them off," I warn for the second time.

Kragen clasps his hands together. "It's out of my control."

Leaping from the deck of the ship, I land in front of Brittney's dirt-covered minivan.

"Elsbeth, how...how did you do that? Did you just jump from the ship?"

"Brittney, you have to leave, now!" I demand. "Don't stop for any reason. Do you understand?"

One of Kragen's men moves behind her at vampire speed, teeth bared. I slam into him before he reaches her, pushing him into the trunk of a heavy oak tree. Her scream pierces the air. "What is that?" she starts.

"Go, now!" The vampire in my arms is fighting against me. He's transformed into a monster, losing all aspects of his humanness.

Brittney doesn't hesitate. She's inside the van with tires spinning within seconds. The moment the van is out of sight, I grab the vampire's head, ripping it from his torso. He collapses in a thud.

"Bravo, my dear," Kragen says from the deck after watching the spectacle I put on. "It seems I underestimated you through the years. Think of all the entertainment I've missed."

"Tell your men to back off," I warn, ignoring his attempt at humor.

"What would be the fun in that?"

"Tell them," I repeat. "I will kill them all."

"Oh, very well. Leave the woman alone." His words are no louder than normal speech, but I know without asking, they will follow orders. "Come back to the ship, my dear. I have something for you."

I could run. I could be back in Charleston in a matter of hours, but I know from experience, Kragen will not leave me alone. Especially now that he finds me...interesting. I jump back to the ship and to the side of my captor. A vampire I don't recognize comes from below deck. He stands in front of me, holding a large white box.

"This is for you," Kragen says as the young vampire pushes the box toward me. Sliding the top off, I'm not surprised to find a wedding dress neatly folded inside.

The young man sets the box on the floor and lifts the dress in front of me. "This will look perfect on you. The color will be perfect with your chestnut hair." The style of the dress reminds me of my youth. Ivory silk taffeta, covered in ruffles and lace, would've been perfect three hundred years ago for the wedding I was never allowed to have.

"It's lovely. Thank you."

"I'm pleased you like it. The wedding will take place before the games begin." Kragen turns to the young man. "See that she's ready by then."

"Today? You said the wedding was Friday."

"Did I? Seems I had my days wrong." He turns, leaving the two of us alone on the deck.

The young vampire throws the dress over his shoulder, looking me up and down. "Seems we have some work to do. Your hair is beautiful, but that style will never do." He claps loudly. "Let's go."

I subconsciously run a hand through what's left of my braid. "What time will the games begin?"

"Oh, I don't know. Whenever Kragen decides for them to begin, but usually around sunset. The setting sun gives a certain ambiance to the hunt." He grabs my hand, pulling me into the captain's quarters. "Have a seat. I have my work cut out for me."

"Who are you?"

"My name is Gordon, and I am your personal stylist for the day. Think of me as your vampire bestie." He smiles, filling me with dread.

Is this guy for real? "Nothing personal, Gordon, but I'm not interested in having a vampire bestie."

"Then I hope you're prepared to deal with the wrath of Kragen because I'm not. Now, sit down, and let's do something to keep him happy. Shall we?"

I'm older and stronger than Gordon and could easily overpower him. Instead of fighting, I choose to follow directions. Maybe he'll have information that will help free the humans.

He pulls out my braid, setting my dark curls free. They hang halfway down my back. "Damn, girl. Your hair *is* beautiful. Why did you keep it hidden in that braid?" He pulls a bag of goodies out of nowhere and begins brushing through the curls, finding every tangle along the way.

"Have you been to one of these before?" I ask.

"A wedding?"

"Kragen's games?"

He laughs. "Oh. Of course. They're something he hosts regularly around here."

"How long do they last?"

Gordon pulls a curling wand from the same bag the brush was in and begins working his magic. "That depends on the quality of product he's acquired."

"You mean how fast the humans run," I correct.

He laughs, making my stomach turn. "That's the best part. Watching them run for their lives. Begging for us to let them live one more minute," he mocks their words, using a baby's voice. I close my eyes to prevent the anger from showing.

Gordon keeps curling, oblivious to my energy shift. "How many vampires will be hunting?"

He shrugs. "Depends on the package they purchased." He stops curling and looks me in the eyes. "Once, there was an entire clan from South America that purchased Kragen's services." He sighs at the memory. "There were some hot Latinos in that mix. Oh, the memories." He continues working on my hair. "Why so many questions?"

"I'm just curious." I wait a few minutes before continuing. "Does Kragen always hold a wedding as part of the games?"

"No, girl. You're the first. To be honest, I thought he was gay and was a little put out that he didn't want me. I mean, look at him, and look at me. Kragen is pretty hot, but then again, so am I. *You* must be something special."

Shit. "I'm nothing special."

"There. Look at that hair, won't you? Kragen is going to want to consummate your marriage on the main deck in front of everyone."

He'll have to kill me first. "How many vampires are here on the ship? I counted eight the other day, but wasn't sure I saw everyone."

"Well," he pulls a box of makeup out of the bag and moves in front of me. "You're right. You didn't see everyone. Last count, there were twenty."

"Twenty," I repeat. There's no way Bert and I can take on twenty vampires, even with the help of the three he knows about.

With no more questions to ask, I sit quietly while Gordon drones on about his life in New Orleans before Kragen found him. My mind plays over every possible outcome of today, all ending in death.

"Voila!" Gordon interrupts my thoughts, shoving a handheld mirror in front of me. "Perfection, if I do say so myself."

The woman staring back at me is pretending to be something she's not. Although her makeup and hair are flawless, the sadness behind her eyes says more than the outside image ever could.

"Our guests should be arriving soon," Gordon says, helping me into the different layers of the dress. The corset he insisted I wear is so tight that it would cut off circulation if I were still human.

He steps back from his creation, clapping his hands. "Perfection. You have to tell me everything that happens after the games. I mean blow by blow...if you know what I mean." He winks, making me want to punch him.

The sound of heavy machinery echoes through the room. "It sounds like our treasure is here." Gordon gathers all of the tools he used. "That means our guests of honor will be arriving soon, and the games will begin."

"What time is it?" I ask.

"Does it matter?" He shrugs and leaves without another word. There's no way Bert and I can take on twenty vampires. I will save as many humans as possible, but I have no qualms about the fact that tonight will be my last. No matter what happens, I will go down fighting.

yo-ho, yo-ho, a pirate's life for me

THE DOOR OPENS, and Kragen enters, wearing a captain's uniform that rivals mine in age. Compared to the costume he wore to greet the French visitors, this one is authentic and perfect. The royal blue long coat looks to be made from velvet and is the perfect accent to the stark white linen shirt underneath. His normally dark hair is covered by a white wig with braids tied throughout. He looks like the iconic pirate I've seen depicted in movies and books throughout the years.

"You look quite lovely, my dear." He holds his hand toward me. "We will make a fine couple."

I have no idea how I'm getting out of this, but there's no way in hell I'm marrying Kragen. I smile, laying my hand on top of his, and allow him to lead me from the room onto the main deck. "Where is everyone?" I ask, looking around the empty ship.

"The wedding will take place on land. Shall we join

them?" Together, we jump from the deck to the shore edge where a group of vampires is beginning to gather.

"Where is the treasure?" I ask, looking around.

"That is none of your concern."

I pull away from his hold. "That *is* my concern. Where is the treasure?"

"They're over there," Gordon answers, nodding his head toward a portable storage building that wasn't there earlier. He giggles as he nods. "This is going to be so much fun. A wedding and a hunt. All the makings of a perfect evening."

Several minutes pass before the remaining vampires join us. With the addition of the French crew, I count twenty-four. Shit. That's too many.

The moment I see Bertram, my heart stops. I'm willing to sacrifice my life for these humans, but I won't allow him to do the same.

"Oh, look. Your family's here," Kragen says, seeing Bert. "He's going to walk you down the aisle."

"There isn't an aisle."

"Semantics," he repeats my words from earlier.

"What a lovely bride," the shorter French vampire says. "A vision of beauty."

"I want to speak to my brother," I announce to the small group. "We need time to catch up."

"I'm afraid that won't be possible." Kragen snaps his fingers, and three vampires I don't recognize come from the wooded area, carrying the bodies of three others. They throw the bodies in a heap not far away.

"Are these the men you are hoping to speak to Bertram about?"

My eyes grow large at the understanding of who the bodies are. The three vampires Bert mentioned during our conversation. Bert's eyes close in recognition of what's happened. "What did you do?" I ask, staring at the two of them.

"I would think that is obvious." Kragen straightens the flowery cuffs of his shirt. "But since it's your wedding day, I will indulge you." He kicks the legs of one of the men. "I had them killed. The mere fact that your brother is still alive is due to his help in identifying these traitors."

"Bertram?"

"Aye," he answers.

"You told him?"

"I had no choice."

My mind reels through the information I shared with him. I told him about Thorne. Dammit. My brother betrayed me.

"You always have a choice," I spew. "After everything?"

"What everything? You're the reason I'm a vampire in the first place. If I hadn't gone looking for you, none of this would've ever happened. I would've married a voluptuous young American woman and had a brood of children. Now, what do I have to look forward to? Eating rodents, chasing terrified humans? What kind of life is that, Bethie?"

"You don't get to call me that," I spew, anger filling me. "I trusted you." I fight the tears from escaping.

"That was your fault," he answers. "I'm sorry I wasn't as good as the perfect Charles. I was never able to fill his shoes. Nothing I did was ever good enough for anyone."

"You did this because of some deep-seated childhood trauma? We all have fucking trauma, Bert. It's how we use that trauma that makes us into the people we are today. If you want to sit around and feel sorry for yourself for the rest of your life, then so be it. That's not me."

"I didn't do this to hurt you. It's me I want to hurt," he argues.

"What are you talking about?"

"I want to die, Elsie."

Kragen claps his hands loudly. "I can make that happen."

"No." I move between my brother and Kragen. "Leave him alone."

"Did you hear the same whining performance that I did? Yet you're still trying to protect him?" Kragen laughs. "Protect the brother who sold you out?"

"Aye," I answer.

"Very well." Kragen steps away from the two of us. "It's time for the ceremony."

He leads me to the makeshift altar, which in actuality is nothing more than branches from a live oak tree twisted together. He pulls away, leaving me alone, before motioning to the shorter French vampire.

The man steps in front of me and smiles deeply. "You look beautiful, wife."

Wife? What the hell? "What is he talking about?"

The French vampire slaps me across the face, the force pushing me into one of the trees behind me. "Don't speak to him," he warns. "You are mine, now."

Kragen smiles, showing the monstrous teeth I remember from years ago. "Did you think *we* were getting married?" He laughs deeply.

"No, my dear. You have been bought and very well paid for, I might say. What happens to you next is not my concern...nor has it ever been."

"You son of a bitch!" I turn toward my soon-to-be husband. "I will not marry you," I spew.

His face transforms into something from nightmares. "Perform the ceremony."

I turn, ripping the skirt from the dress, and hear an audible gasp from Gordon not far behind me. I continue ripping until reaching the pantaloons that all women wore underneath heavy dresses during that time period.

I turn away from the ensuing chaos with the intention of freeing as many humans as possible. Fuck the wedding, fuck Kragen, and fuck my future husband. I move vampire speed when an energy I'd recognize anywhere hits me square in the chest. I stop, turning toward the source, and hear a voice that brings tears to my eyes.

"I'm here, and I'm not alone," Thorne's voice whispers through my mind from somewhere out of sight. I don't know how he communicated through my mind, but I'm not questioning it.

Turning back toward the wedding party, I'm surprised to see no one has moved. In fact, my groom looks quite bored with the situation. "Are you finished?" Kragen asks.

"No." I laugh. "I'm just getting started." Seconds later, I'm standing in front of the treasure box full of terrified humans. Breaking open the lock, I open the doors wide. In front of me is an image that will haunt me for the rest of my life.

Human children are huddled in the back of the unit. They're filthy and wearing nothing but rags. As soon as the door opens, they cower further against the walls. "It's okay, you're safe," I lie.

"It looks like your bride is starting the games early," Kragen announces.

"I'm out of the mood to marry that bitch now," my French friend adds. "I'll expect a full refund." The visitor raises his nose high in the air. "Does anyone else smell dog?"

Kragen and the crew of vampires behind him copy his movements, lifting their noses to the sky, smelling the same scent. I smile, knowingly.

"What have you done, my dear?" Kragen asks, a

wide smile covering his face. "This just got more interesting."

"I've done nothing, *my dear,* but I'm excited to see the outcome."

I feel their energy before I see them. They're all around me. Not only do I feel Thorne, but an overwhelming amount of lycan energy fills the woods nearby. I wedge the door tight, hoping to keep the children safe for a while longer.

Thorne moves to my side seconds later, lacing his fingers through mine. "Hello, beautiful."

"God, I'm glad to see you."

"Sorry it took so long. We got lost a few times."

I turn, facing the man I love. He's wearing the same clothes as the day I left, and his hair is a disheveled mess. "Your timing is impeccable."

He smiles, looking me up and down. "It seems you've been busy."

"Captain Hawthorne Rex, I believe," Kragen greets Thorne. "I don't remember extending an invitation to the games, but who am I to argue?" He lifts his hands to the side. "The more, the merrier."

"Glad to hear it, Kragen. I brought a few of my friends."

As he speaks, three vampires I don't recognize step on the other side of Thorne. Two men who dwarf Thorne and a woman with coal black hair join our fight. "Elsie, this is Abram, Elias, and Samirah."

"Hello," they greet in unison.

"Thank you for coming."

Samirah laughs. "Thorne wouldn't take no for an answer."

On cue, a symphony of howls echoes through the woods behind us. "Connor brought a few friends as well," Thorne adds.

"Free the treasure!" I yell toward Kragen.

"I'm growing bored with this," he answers. "It doesn't matter how many dogs or weak vampires you brought, you don't stand a chance."

"Bertram is with Kragen," I whisper to Thorne.

"Your brother, Bertram?"

"Aye. No one is to harm him."

"Understood," the vampires answer in unison again, making me wonder if they're some strange sort of triplets.

"You'll have to go through us to reach the treasure," I issue a threat to Kragen and the French boys.

"That sounds like fun," my French ex-future husband answers. "What do you think, Pierre?" he asks the taller of the two.

"Agreed, Jon Paul. It's been a few centuries since we've participated in such doings." The two men's, along with the vampires they brought with them, eyes turn solid black, as their faces contort.

"Here they come," Samirah whispers as the group begins moving.

Out of nowhere, a wolf appears on my other side. Without asking, I know that it's Micah. Large green eyes look into mine before he leaps on top of one of the younger French vampires, ripping its head from its torso without much effort.

A group of wolves moves from behind the wedding party. A smaller wolf makes the first move, jumping on Gordon, she copies Micah's movement from earlier, tearing his head from his body.

Grabbing a small branch from one of the oak trees, I run toward several of Kragen's younger vampires, piercing their hearts before they know what happened. Both collapse to the ground instantly.

The sounds of a war raging fill the air as lycan appear from seemingly nowhere, taking out the weaker vampires first. Kragen, Pierre, and Jon Paul watch in amusement as the fight ensues around them.

Setting my sights on the French guests first, I move vampire speed in front of them. Two younger vampires are standing in front of their makers, acting as their personal guards. I smirk at the irony. "You let your children protect you?"

"That's what they're for," Pierre answers.

"They're expendable," Jon Paul adds.

I move faster than eyes can track, jumping behind the young vampire guarding Pierre and ripping his head from his body. "One down, one to go," I tease. Pierre doesn't look fazed that I just killed his guard.

Copying my moves from earlier, I do the same to the one guarding Jon Paul, leaving the two French aristocrats unguarded and alone. "Well done," Jon Paul says with a yawn. "Now what?"

"Now, it's your turn."

Pierre steps in front of Jon Paul. "Dear girl, do you know how old we are? Even you, with your pretentious puppy dog parade, don't stand a chance against the likes of us. My name is Pierre Dubois, and I am over five hundred years old."

"Congratulations?"

"Imbecile," Jon Paul continues. Faster than my eyes can track, movement happens behind both of the ancient vampires. In the blink of an eye, their heads are severed from their bodies and lying on the ground at their feet. What the hell just happened?

It takes a few minutes to connect the dots. Kragen is standing near them, his face covered in dark blood. "Those two were annoying," he says, wiping a dark stain on the crisp white shirt. "Besides, I offer no refunds." He straightens his coat and cuffs. "It's time for this to end. Call them off."

"No."

He looks up, completely confused by the word foreign to his vocabulary.

"Elsie, you're not going to survive this," Bert says from behind Kragen. "None of you will. Is it worth it?"

"I would rather die than be Kragen's slave any longer."

"Is it worth it to lose the captain?" he nods toward Thorne, who just killed two of Kragen's men.

"Thorne makes his own decisions," I retort.

In the time the three of us have been talking, the lycan and vampires with Thorne have destroyed all of the French vampires' men, along with Kragen's. All that's left are he and Bert.

"Your men are dead, Kragen. You're outnumbered and out manpowered. You're not going to survive this."

Kragen laughs. "I have been outnumbered before, my dear." He turns toward Bert, grabs my brother's arm, and jumps both of them to the deck of the ship. Seconds later, two explosions rock the shore, throwing the lycan and vampire to the ground.

Thorne is at my side instantly. "Are you okay?"

"I'm fine." I stand, brushing the sand mixture from my face. "He's got Bert." We stand in awe as the sails rise on the pirate ship, filling with wind, and taking the ship toward the Atlantic.

"This just got more interesting," Micah says from beside me. He's in human form and doesn't seem fazed by the fact that he's naked.

"Aye, it did," Thorne adds.

The next few hours are spent cleaning up any remnants of the fight and dealing with the human victims. When all is said and done, surprisingly, only one lycan was injured. I don't know how or why everyone survived, but I'm not questioning it.

"That has to be the slowest escape in the history of escapes," Luna says, coming to my side. "We could stop them in minutes." The two of us stare at the disappearing sails of the ancient ship as it disappears into the ocean beyond. "It's not like he can outrun us or sneak away."

"No, but I don't doubt that anyone who tries to board that ship will die."

"Yeah, I figured." She reaches an arm around me, pulling me close. "You were amazing out there. You're pretty badass."

I smile, not used to receiving compliments. "Thank you. You're pretty badass yourself." I nod toward the now empty storage unit. "How are the kids?"

She shrugs. "Traumatized, but alive. I can't imagine what they've been through. They'll have a rough road ahead of them, but they're going to be okay. Brittney's on her way with several local police officials to help."

On cue, a white minivan pulls to a stop. "Oh, my God," Brittney exclaims, climbing out of her car. She runs to me, wrapping her thin arms behind my back. "I'm so glad you're alive."

"Brittney told me where you were," Thorne interrupts, coming to my side. "If it weren't for her, we wouldn't have gotten here in time."

I hug her a second time. "Thank you, Brittney."

"You're welcome, sugar. Now, where are those babies I need to look at?" Two ambulances and several police cars arrive, parking behind the minivan. "The cavalry's here," she says, moving toward the huddled and terrified children.

"The lycan have fulfilled their end of our bargain," Connor says, moving beside our small group.

Thorne shakes the large man's hand. "Thank you, my friend. We couldn't have done it without you."

"I'd like to see this through," Micah says to his father. "This isn't over." He nods toward the ship that's nearly out of sight.

The Alpha nods, giving his son permission to stay. "Be careful."

"I'm staying, too," Luna adds. "That son of a bitch doesn't deserve to live."

why me?

"HE ESCAPED IN A PIRATE SHIP?" Francis asks, for the fourth time. "A real pirate ship?

"Aye," Thorne answers. "The same one he had three hundred years ago." Francis has been asking him questions since we returned to Charleston a few hours ago.

Pictures of Kragen's ship have been plastered all over social media, as people follow the journey of the pirate down the Outer Banks of North Carolina. To humans, it's a spectacle. To me, it's a threat.

"He's coming here," Luna says, watching the latest news broadcast featuring the ship. "He's going to park the damn thing in Charleston and come for a visit."

"This is so exciting," Francis exclaims. "I get to be part of the action."

"Would he seriously be dumb enough to come here?" Micah asks.

"Yes," Thorne and I answer in unison.

The doorbell rings and Francis scurries towards the door, returning moments later with the three vampires from the Outer Banks. "It seems you have some friends," Francis says, bringing them into the room.

"Abram, Elias, Samirah," Thorne greets the vampires with a nod. "Thank you for coming."

"Abram suggested you might need our help," Samirah answers, nodding toward the man with striking features. His skin is coffee-colored, while his eyes are pale blue. The contrast between the two is beautiful together.

"We're here to see this through," Abram answers. "That was the most fun I've had in decades." He smiles, moving closer. "Abram Davis." He holds his hand toward me. "I'm afraid we weren't properly introduced before."

"Elsbeth Abernathy," I answer, shaking his large hand.

"How do you three know Thorne?"

The other man, Elias, smiles before answering. "It's a long story."

"It seems we have plenty of time," Francis answers, pointing at the slow-moving ship plastered across the television.

"We're from Savannah."

"Oh, what a beautiful city," Francis interrupts. "I've been there many times."

"It is," Elias continues. "Several years ago, we had a bit of trouble with a young vampire. The young man became obsessed with a young lycan female who didn't return his affection."

"A fatal attraction type thing?" Luna asks.

Elias smiles, clearly not understanding her famous movie reference. "The young woman was the daughter of the Alpha and didn't want to be with the vampire."

"To make a long story short," Samirah interrupts. "Nothing personal, Elias, but we all know you enjoy the sound of your own voice." She winks at the blonde vampire. "The vampire didn't take it well and threatened to expose both communities to the unsuspecting humans. Thorne helped us *resolve* the issue."

"That sounds familiar," Luna adds, nudging Thorne with her shoulder. "Maybe that's where you came up with the idea?"

"No matter the reason, thank you for your help. I'm not sure we could've done it without you," I answer.

"What is that vampire to you?" Samirah asks from across the room.

"My maker," I answer truthfully.

"He's the asshole that kidnapped her three hundred years ago off my ship," Thorne adds.

"He kidnapped you?" Samirah questions.

"Yeah. I escaped a hundred years later and have been on the run ever since."

"That's horrible. I'm sorry that happened to you," Elias answers for the group.

"So, let's go storm the pirate ship and kick his ass," Francis says, standing behind the vampires.

"You're human?" Elias asks the elderly woman, already knowing the answer.

Francis stands a little straighter. "I am." She looks at Thorne. "He's my great-great-great-grandfather."

Samirah smiles widely. "Is that for real?"

"Aye," Thorne answers, matching her smile. "I am."

"Is there a plan for the ship and Kragen?" Abram asks as he sits on the overstuffed couch.

I share a look with Thorne. "No," I answer truthfully. As far as we know, Kragen and Bertram are the only two aboard. Whoever tries to step foot on board will be killed."

"But you think he's coming here?" Samirah asks.

"Aye," Thorne chimes in.

"Why? What's so special about Charleston?" Elias joins the conversation.

"It's not the city," I answer. "It's me. He's chased me for nearly two hundred years."

"Please don't take this the wrong way, but what is so special about *you*?" Abram asks the question I've wondered for centuries.

I shrug. "I don't know. I've asked the same question through the years."

Thorne moves to my side and pulls me close. "He's not going to get to you again."

"Maybe she needs to go to him," Samirah volunteers.

"Hell, no," Thorne interrupts.

"What do you have in mind, Samirah?" I ask.

"I found something while you were gone," Francis interrupts. "It didn't make much sense until now." She moves toward a large book on the edge of the dining room table. "This is one of the books that have been in the house for centuries. I don't know where it came from, to be honest, or what made me look through it while you were gone, but something grabbed my attention." She opens it to a paper sticking out of the end and begins skimming over the page. "Here." She points, reading out loud.

"Those cursed by Eudora are bound to walk the earth and sea for all eternity."

"What's a Eudora?" Micah asks.

Francis flips through a few more pages to an image of an older woman, surrounded by raging seas, with her hair and clothing blowing in the wind. "Eudora is a sea witch. This is her."

"A sea witch?" Luna interrupts. "Like from the Disney movie? The one who stole Ariel's voice?"

"According to what I've read, witches take on many forms and elements. A sea witch lives in or near water," Francis answers, ignoring Luna's question. "Some are stronger than others, and a few wield powers from other worlds."

"Yep, like the Disney movie." Luna folds her arms over her chest.

"Meaning that Eudora must be very strong," Samirah adds.

"Aye. A person bound to walk the earth and sea for all eternity sounds like a vampire," Thorne says what I'm thinking.

"What does this have to do with Kragen and his obsession with me?" I ask, not sure where this is leading.

Francis continues reading.

"Those cursed by the witch can only die through the hands of a female offspring."

"What does that mean?" Elias asks. "A female offspring? Vampires can't have children."

"No, but they can create them." Thorne fills in the blanks. He turns toward me. "Besides you, did Kragen create any other female vampires?"

"Not that I saw, but a lot could've happened in two hundred years, or for that matter, before I was made."

"There's more," Francis says, interrupting.

"The cursed or those cursed by him will not be permitted to harm the female."

"In other words, Kragen or any of his creations cannot kill you," Abram translates.

"That's all well and good, but what's to keep

someone much older than him from ending his life?" Micah asks.

"Nothing," I answer. "What are the chances of finding a vampire that is older and is willing to kill Kragen?"

"Slim," Thorne answers. "Viktor was ancient, but he's no longer on Earth. We have no idea how old Kragen is."

"I do," I whisper to the crowd in the room. "He told me once." I look up to see every pair of eyes patiently waiting for me to continue. "He was born in Brittania during the first century."

"The first century?" Micah repeats. "That makes him over two thousand years old."

Thorne turns toward me. "I mean no offense, but how could you overtake someone that strong?"

"I couldn't," I answer truthfully. "I can't."

Luna stands, moving to the center of the room. "Okay, am I the only one who needs a recap?" She takes a deep breath. "Kragen is old, like old as fuck." She turns toward Francis, "I'm sorry, Ms. Francis." Francis waves her hand in dismissal. "Kragen is old," she continues. "The sea witch who turned him into a vampire cursed him so that only one of his female creations could kill him? Does this sound right so far?" The room nods in agreement. "Then why would he marry you off to that French asshole? Why not just hire someone to kill you? I doubt money is an issue for him.

It seems out of character for him to bring you onto his ship just to marry you off."

Luna's right. It doesn't make any sense.

"Maybe he doesn't want to kill her. Maybe he wants to be the one to die," Francis says from behind the large book. "Maybe he's ready to die, and Elsie is the only person on Earth capable of doing it."

"That's insane," Elias argues. "I've heard stories of this lunatic forever. I've never met a vampire who wanted to die."

"You've never met a vampire as old as he is," Francis argues.

"Then why all the theatrics?" I ask the room.

"Everything Kragen does is for attention. Why would his death be any different?" Thorne answers.

"He knew you'd come to rescue me." I put the puzzle pieces together. "The ship was all part of his plan. He wanted things to happen just the way they did."

"Then we need to keep up with his plan," Micah says. "No doubt he's waiting for you to come looking for him. You need to oblige him," Micah repeats Samirah's words from earlier.

"They're right," I agree. Thorne rubs a hand through his hair, sighing deeply with my words. "If he's ready to die, I need to give him what he wants."

"What if everyone's wrong? What if he kills you? You don't stand a chance against him if he puts up a fight."

"He's not going to," Francis says, sitting down. "I may not be chronologically the oldest person in this room, but I'm in the oldest vessel. I know what it's like to want to die. I know what it's like to have nothing to look forward to or live for." She pauses before continuing. "If Kragen's truly ready to die, then he's not going to fight. Hell, he's bringing a damn pirate ship with him as he comes. It's not like he's sneaking down the coast. He's not hiding anything."

Thorne sits next to his granddaughter. "I'm sorry you've felt like that in your life." He wraps an arm around her shoulders.

"Let her go to him," Francis continues.

Thorne closes his eyes in response. "What if?"

"No," she interrupts. "There are no what ifs. I'm right about this."

He looks up at me, tears welling in his eyes. "Are you sure about this?"

Am I sure about this? No, but I don't dare answer truthfully. "Aye," I lie instead.

"Tomorrow then." Thorne stands, moves to my side, and pulls me close. "Tonight, the lycan need to rest."

"And the human," Francis adds.

"You're not going with us," Thorne starts.

"Like hell, I'm not. Even if it's to watch from the banks of the Ashley River, I'm going. I may never get another chance to see a sight like this again. Putting my eyes on an actual pirate ship is a life goal. You can't deny me that."

Francis stands, turning toward her guests. "I know you don't require a place to sleep, but there are rooms upstairs with fresh linens if you'd like to lie down, and I have some clothing that's been left here throughout the years that might fit a few of you if you'd like to clean up a little."

"Thank you," Samirah answers for all of them. "That is very kind of you."

Thorn wraps a protective arm around my shoulders, leading me upstairs to the honeymoon suite. He opens the door, and the familiar scent hits me quickly. I was only here for a few days, but it became more of a home than anywhere I've been in my life.

"This was my room when I built the house," Thorne says, touching the fireplace mantle.

"Francis told me." I move behind him, wrapping my arms around his waist. "I'm going to be okay."

He turns, facing me. "You don't know that."

"No, I don't. But I refuse to think otherwise."

"I can't lose you again, Elsie."

"You won't." My lips crash into his in a frenzy of emotion. He matches my intensity, thrusting his tongue toward mine. The combination threatens to throw me over the edge. Strong hands reach behind my ass, lifting me and pulling me closer to him.

I wrap my legs around him as he carries me toward the bed without losing contact with my lips. Laying me on my back, he pulls away only long enough to take the filthy shirt he's wearing off.

"Get the pants while you're there." I smile with my words.

He follows directions and returns the smile. "You're kind of bossy."

"You know you like it," I retort.

"Aye." He stands in front of me completely naked, and I can't stop staring at the grand prize. Thorne reaches up, wrapping his hands around my thighs, and pulling me closer until the softest part of me meets the hardest part of him with my butt hanging off the side of the mattress. "Why are you still dressed?" he asks, teasing me with his touch.

"Because you were my top priority in the undressing department."

"We'll just have to fix that." He rips the leggings I found in Brittney's minivan with one pull, laying them next to me on the bed. "That's better."

"I liked those." I sit up, pulling my T-shirt and bra off.

"That's even better," Thorne says. His pupils are dilated, and his eyes are full of heat.

I wrap my arms and legs around his neck and waist, slowly lowering myself onto him. We sigh at the contact. Thorne moves his hands to my ass, urging me to move faster as the connection between us grows. "Damn, you feel so good," he whispers into my ear. His words bring chill bumps to the surface.

Without warning, he lowers me to the bed and steps away from the edge. Lifting my legs onto his shoulders, he kisses me in a place that's never been kissed before. Plunging his tongue deeper, he touches the part of me begging to be touched.

An embarrassing sigh escapes as the combination brings me to a full-fledged orgasm within seconds. My body begins to shake with his motions, begging for him to both stop and continue at the same time.

"Oh, my God," I sigh, coming down from the high.

"I'm just getting started." Thorne's words are sexy as hell as my body continues to relax. I want to make him feel as good as I do. As soon as my body settles, I don't ask permission. I lower to the ground, kneeling in front of him, and take every inch of him into my mouth. I slowly begin working my hands in conjunction with my tongue, massaging and sucking at the same time.

Thorne grabs the back of my head, pulling me closer. He begins to move faster, matching the pace of my hands, moving deeper and deeper into my mouth. "You better stop, or this is going to be over quicker than both of us want." He pants.

I pull backward, releasing him from my grip. He bends down, and his mouth finds mine in an instant as he lifts me in front of him again, this time walking with me in his arms until my back touches the wall. Wrapping my legs around his waist, he lowers me slowly, taking his time to allow each inch of him to fill me with desire.

His mouth never leaves mine as he continues to slide in and out slowly, exploring every inch of my body with his tongue and hands. In the three centuries I've been on this planet, I've never felt so alive or loved.

My breathing picks up along with his pace as he continues pushing into me. The smell of copper fills the air as my nails pierce his skin, hoping to pull him even closer to me.

The sensation begins low in my core, filling me even more. "Deeper," I whisper.

He follows directions, pushing until there's no room left to push. Our breathing matches pace as we continue moving in our choreographed dance until we cry out in unison. The overwhelming sensation filling my body is a mixture of love, tears, pain, hunger, and desire.

Thorne continues to shudder as the two of us stay connected. "I love you, Elsie," he breathes into my mouth.

"I love you, too, Captain."

speed demon

A KNOCK on the door pulls me out of the love trance I've been in for the past few hours. "The news just showed Kragen's ship. He's definitely heading here," Micah announces through the door. "My father would like to meet with you both."

"Aye, probably a good idea," Thorne answers, moving away from me. After exploring every inch of each other several times, we've spent the past few hours wrapped in each other's arms, discussing everything except Kragen. "We'll be down in a minute."

"Not until after a shower," I mumble, moving quickly toward the bathroom.

"We'll be down in thirty minutes." Thorne corrects himself before following me to the bathroom.

I turn, realizing he's naked. "If you get in that shower with me, it's going to take longer than thirty minutes before we appear."

Disappointment covers his face. "Aye, you're right."

I stop inches in front of him, grabbing his cock with my hands. "We have centuries to make up for, and I will make up for each day we missed." I kiss him on the end of his nose, before closing the shower door behind me.

"You're killing me," he mutters, closing the bathroom door behind him.

I shower quickly, rehashing everything that's happened in the past week.

Ten minutes later, I'm dressed, and Thorne takes my place under the water. I take longer than usual to style my hair, adding a small amount of makeup to give me a little color.

"There they are," Connor announces as we walk downstairs at exactly thirty minutes on the dot. "I hope you don't mind if we meet here."

"Not at all," Thorne answers.

"What are we going to do about Kragen?" Connor asks, not mincing words. "He can't bring a damn pirate ship into the marina. The tourists will attempt to purchase rides."

"Are you suggesting we meet him while he's still in the Atlantic?" I ask.

Connor moves toward an antique settee. "I don't think we have a choice. Do we know how many are on board?"

"Unless there was someone below deck, it's just Kragen and my brother."

"According to his speed and location, he should be here around sunset tonight."

"Then we need to get to him before then," Thorne answers.

"Micah and I are prepared to fight," Connor says.

I shake my head. "I won't ask the pack to fight for me again. This is between Kragen and me."

"You didn't ask," Micah answers, moving toward the door. "We'll be back in an hour with transportation." The two lycan exit, leaving Thorne and I alone in the room.

"We need a plan," I announce.

"When are we leaving?" Francis asks, joining us. Thorne takes a deep breath, and Francis holds a hand toward his face. "I know what you're going to say. It's useless. I'm coming. If I die out there, it's better than dying alone in here." She stares him down. "I'm not taking no for an answer."

"I can't guarantee your safety," he argues.

"No one asked you to."

"We're all coming," Samirah announces as the small group of vampires and Luna come into the room. "We need to see this through."

"Micah and Connor are returning with what I'm assuming is a boat in an hour," I answer, looking around at the small army of quick friends. "Thank you."

"I'll make some sandwiches," Francis announces, leaving the room.

"Oh, I'll help." Luna follows.

"Does she know we don't eat human food?" Elias whispers.

"Aye, she just wants to feel useful," Thorne answers. "If something happens to me, you must protect her."

"Understood," Elias answers.

Thirty minutes later, Luna drags her phone out of her pocket, reading a text. "Micah says they're at the marina already."

"None of you have to do this." I remind them, looking around the room, and making eye contact with each person. "You don't owe me anything."

"We know," Luna answers, leading the group toward the door.

The marina is several blocks away, and we decide to walk the distance. Noticing Francis straggling behind, Thorne picks her up, carrying her like a bride crossing the threshold. "I could get used to this," she says with a smile.

"You need to eat more. You don't weigh anything."

Francis laughs. "You and your compliments. No wonder you charmed the pants off of that one." She nods toward me, and I feel the redness covering my face. "Oh, don't look embarrassed now. I'm pretty sure everyone in the house heard how many times those pants were charmed off."

"Agreed." Luna adds. "I lost count."

"Oh, my God. I'm sorry." I can't control the smile plastered across my face.

"Didn't sound that way earlier," Luna answers.

"We're here," Samirah interrupts...thankfully.

In the middle of the marina is a boat I recognize from dolphin cruise pamphlets. "Speed Demon" is plastered all over the side of the neon yellow speedboat. Micah waves from the wheel.

"What the hell is that?" Francis asks.

"I'm afraid that is our ride," Luna answers. "Nothing like being inconspicuous."

"This is getting better by the minute," Francis adds as Thorne sets her back on solid ground. The six of us work our way to the boat.

"Did you steal this?" Luna asks, climbing on board.

"It belongs to the pack," Connor answers. "How else do you think we earn money during tourist season?"

"I don't know, a restaurant maybe?" Samirah answers, making me laugh.

"If you're human or lycan, you must wear a life jacket." Micah looks around after his statement. "Insurance requires it."

"Does insurance stipulate that vampires aren't required to wear lifesaving equipment?" Abram asks.

"Not in so many words," he answers.

It doesn't take long to get everyone situated and the proper equipment on everyone except the vampires. Micah pilots the boat out of the marina toward the open sea.

"How far out is he?" Thorne asks.

"Not far in the Atlantic. If he comes any closer, we risk exposure to bystanders," Connor answers.

As soon as we're in open water, Micah pushes the boat faster, throwing everyone backward into their seats.

"Holy shit," Francis exclaims. "No wonder people pay a fortune to ride this thing. I think my soul just left my body."

Thorne moves beside his descendant, pulling her close as she giggles with the waves.

It doesn't take long for the sails of the ship to come into view. "There she is," Micah announces, pulling the boat to a stop. "Before we get closer, what's the plan?"

"Pull the boat alongside. Elsie and I will board alone," Thorne says, acting like the captain he is. "If we need help, we'll call on you."

I have no intention of allowing Thorne to put himself in harm's way. If the prophecy is right, I'm the only person who can kill Kragen. I know Kragen well enough to know he will kill Thorne to force my hand. If Kragen truly wants to die, I will give him what he wants.

Micah seems to accept Thorne's suggestion and moves the boat closer to the ship. The moment we're in range for me to jump to the main deck, I do, leaving Thorne behind.

Landing on the deck of the ship, I'm not surprised to find it empty. "What the hell?" Thorne asks, landing behind me.

"Go back to the boat," I demand. "I don't want you here."

"What are you talking about?"

"I'm talking about this is for me to do alone. I will not allow you to die for me."

"Are you serious? I had myself turned into a fucking vampire for you. There's no way in hell I'm letting you do this alone." Anger rushes off of Thorne.

"I didn't ask you to do that."

"No, you didn't. I did it because I love you, Elsie, and I knew it was the only way to find you."

"You can't leave her alone," I continue, nodding toward the boat. "Francis needs you."

"I'm not leaving her alone, nor am I leaving you alone. Let me help you. It's not necessary to sacrifice yourself for everyone again. I watched you do that once before and will not allow it to happen again."

"Lover's quarrel?" Kragen says from behind me. "What a shame."

"I'm here, Kragen."

"I can both see and hear that," he answers sarcastically.

"What do you want from me?"

He moves closer. "What I want is simple. I want to die."

"I can make sure that happens," Thorne answers.

Kragen rolls his eyes. "You're dumber than I originally thought. You can't kill me, boy. How do you think I've survived this long? Skill? Strength?"

"You're immortal," I answer.

"Yes, that's true, but so are you," he answers. "I'm guessing that since you've come to me, you discovered the curse placed on me."

"Aye," I answer.

Kragen opens his arms wide, exposing his chest. "Then I'm ready, my dear."

"Why?"

"Why do I want to die?"

"No, why me? Why would you turn me knowing I would be able to kill you one day?"

"Guilt? Pity? Self-loathing? Any of those emotions will fill in the blank." He moves closer toward Thorne. "It's fitting that your captain be here to see this. After all, he's the reason I found you in the first place."

"I know the reason you found Elsbeth. My first officer sold information to your men. He admitted the truth right before I killed him."

Kragen laughs. "That imbecile couldn't find his asshole from his nose. He wasn't even capable of finding one of my men to speak with. No, Captain, *you're* the reason I took Elsbeth. The burden lies solely with you."

"What are you talking about?" Thorne asks.

"Do you remember the sea creature your men brought on board not long before you picked up Elsbeth's family?"

Thorne looks confused. "You'll have to be more specific, Kragen. My men did quite a bit of fishing."

"Your men thought she was sick. They pulled her in with their nets."

"The injured dolphin?" Thorne asks, connecting the dots.

"That's the one," Kragen confirms.

"My men put it out of its misery. She was deformed and dying."

"Your men *killed* her," Kragen shouts. For the first time since I've known him, he loses his demeanor.

"My men killed a sick dolphin. What does that have to do with you taking Elsie?"

"That was no dolphin, Captain." Spit flies from his mouth as he speaks. "That dolphin was Eudora," Kragen answers, his voice softer.

"Eudora? The sea witch? The one that turned you into a vampire?" I ask, remembering the book Francis read from.

"*She* was my wife. That dolphin was my wife."

"You were married to Eudora?"

"For many years," he adds. "We were lovers in *all* sense of the word." Kragen gets lost in a memory. "She often took on the form of sea animals when she swam. A dolphin was one of her favorites." Tears form in his eyes. "Your men dragged her on board, and you ordered her death, Captain."

"I...I didn't realize," Thorne answers.

"Of course, you didn't. You were only a stupid mortal." He looks at me. "That's why I took *her*."

"You took me because Eudora died?"

Kragen closes his eyes. "She didn't just die, my dear. She was murdered."

"I'm sorry—" Thorne starts.

"Save your meaningless apologies for someone else. Your words mean nothing," Kragen interrupts.

"Kragen, I'm sorry for Eudora, but what did that have to do with me?" I ask the obvious question.

"Someone had to suffer. Why not take the man responsible for her death's true love? After all, he took mine. It was the perfect revenge."

"Then why turn me into a vampire? Why not kill me in front of him?"

Kragen smiles, lifting one side of his mouth higher than the other. "Torture is so much more convincing. What's the point of torturing your human body for a few short weeks, or possibly a month, when I can make that torture last an eternity?" He turns toward Thorne. "Imagine my surprise when I discovered your true love had sought after and succeeded in turning himself into one of us. What is the saying? Two birds with one stone?"

"Eudora cursed you to walk the earth for eternity, only able to die at the hands of a woman you created. What kind of love was that?" I spew.

"You know nothing, young one."

"Enlighten us," Thorne interrupts.

"An eternity with Eudora, with my true love was all I ever wanted. All I ever needed. Your men found her during transformation when she was at her weakest.

When you ordered her death, you killed me along with her."

"You want to join her," I fill in the blanks for him.

Kragen closes his eyes. "Yes."

"What makes you think I'll grant your wishes?"

He smiles widely. "Because you'll do anything for love. You've proven that many times."

"And because I'll kill him," a voice says behind me. I turn, finding Bertram's large arm locked around Thorne's throat, pointing a wooden stake straight at Thorne's heart.

"Bert? What are you doing?"

"Following the orders of my maker. Something you should be doing, too."

"Bertram, step away from Thorne," I warn.

"Why?" he asks. His pupils are dilated, and his face is flushed as the tip of the stake pierces Thorne's skin, bringing blood to the surface.

"You don't have to follow his orders. You can come with me, with us."

Tears fill Bert's eyes. "You just want Charles."

"Charles is dead. You're not. I want to be with you. There's time to live our lives together—time that was stolen from us by him." I point at Kragen.

"*You* stole that life from me," Bert argues.

I stare at my brother, not sure how to help him. "Kragen stole both of our lives. He killed Charles. All three of us are his victims. Don't let him have this power over you."

"She's angry because you're not as perfect as your older brother," Kragen continues his brainwashing. "She wishes it was Charles who was still alive, not you. You were a weak and needy child. Always a burden. In fact, if it weren't for you, I would have never seen the love between these two." He nods toward Thorne and me.

"Shut up, Kragen," I retort.

"He deserves to know the truth, Elsbeth."

"Bert, don't listen to him. His truth isn't real. I love you. I've always loved you."

My younger brother wipes a tear. "Kragen's right." He shoves the stake even further into Thorne's chest, moving closer to his heart.

Movement behind them catches my eye. Crouched low and moving quickly is the shadow of Samirah. I know Kragen sees her too, but he doesn't acknowledge her. She's heading straight toward Bert and Thorne.

"Bert, let him go," I warn.

"Do my master's bidding," he answers. "Take his life."

I turn toward Kragen, whose arms are spread out to the side, with his chest bared. "I'm ready, my dear."

I hear Samirah before I see her. In what sounds like a whoosh of sound, I turn just as she leaps onto the back of Bertram, teeth bared.

"No!" I shout just as she bites into my brother's neck, separating his head from his body.

It takes a few minutes for the realization of what

just happened to sink in. My brother's head is lying on the deck next to his now collapsed body. He's dead. Bertram is dead.

"What did you do?" I scream toward the crouched body of Samirah.

"He was going to kill Thorne," she answers, moving in front of me. "That wasn't okay."

"He wasn't going to kill him," I argue. "He was just a confused little boy."

"He was a whole ass vampire," she says, matching my energy. "There wasn't a little boy left anywhere inside of him. You're a fool if you think otherwise."

I wipe the tears flowing down my cheek. "He was the only thing I had left."

"I'm sorry about that, but I wasn't willing to risk Thorne's life."

Looking between the two of them, I see a connection that I was stupid to not see earlier. Something passes between them, and I know without asking, they're lovers. "How can I have been so blind?"

Thorne closes his eyes, looking at the wooden deck below. "It's not what it seems, Elsie."

"You're going to stand there, next to my dead brother's body, and tell me that the two of you are not lovers?"

He sighs. "That's not important right now."

"It seemed important enough for her to kill my brother."

"Well done, my dear," Kragen says from behind me.

Samirah smiles, moving from behind Thorne and to Kragen's side. "Thank you, my love." She reaches up, kissing him on the lips. What the ever-living hell just happened?

"Samirah?" Thorne asks, looking just as confused as I feel.

"Why do you look so shocked?" she asks. "Kragen and I found each other years ago. We've been lovers ever since. You were just a stop along the way."

Facing Kragen, I let every bit of rage and anger flow. "I'm ready to kill you now."

Kragen laughs, pulling Samirah close. "Maybe later."

"Am I the only one that's confused?" I ask whoever is listening.

"You were right. That was fun," Samirah says from his side.

"I told you, my dear." He reaches down, kissing her again. "Wreaking havoc is what life's all about." He turns toward me. "I'm always one step ahead, my dear. It's all part of the game. Shall we take our leave?"

"We shall," she answers as the two of them lift into the sky, leaving Thorne and me alone on the deck.

ships, poems, and death

"WHAT JUST HAPPENED?" Elias asks, landing on the main deck. "Did Kragen take Samirah?"

"I don't think there was any *taking* to it. She went willingly," I answer.

"What the hell?" Abram adds. "Why would she do that?"

"Because they're lovers," I answer, glaring in Thorne's direction.

Micah climbs over the side of the railing with Francis thrown over his shoulder, followed by Luna and Connor. He sets her down carefully. "Did he take Samirah?" she asks, propping her hands on her hips.

I repeat the story for the small audience, ending with Kragen taking off the deck with Samirah in his arms.

"What's next?" Francis asks as the group stands

around, absorbing the overload of information. "Do we go after him?"

"Aye," Thorne answers.

I kneel next to what's left of my younger brother. Bertram's body is already starting to disintegrate, returning to the dust from which it came. "I'm so sorry, sweet Bert. I wish I could've helped you."

"You did everything you could," Thorne says, coming to my side.

"Not to ignore the obvious, but what are we going to do with this damn thing?" Francis motions to the pirate ship.

"We need to get it to port. I don't know how to sail something like this," Connor says.

"I do." Thorne stands. "I know how to sail it." He moves quickly to the helm, turning the wheel back toward the city of Charleston. "I need the lycan to man one sail while Elias and Abram man the other. As we move into port, you're going to have to lower them when I tell you."

"How do we do that?" Elias asks, moving toward the first set of sails.

"I know how...I think," Micah answers. "Switch with me. Between the four of us, we can figure it out."

"I know what to do," Francis announces. She moves between the two teams. "Tell me when you're ready," she yells toward the helm.

"Why does this feel sketchy?" Luna asks.

"Because it is," I answer.

We enter the river, pass Fort Sumter, and move closer to the main port of Charleston. Tourists at the fort have already noticed us and are either pointing or staring at the huge pirate ship passing next to them. Small boats begin following the ship as we move further into port.

I move next to Thorne. "Think this thing will fit?"

He huffs a laugh. "Things have changed quite a bit from when I did this before, but I think she'll fit." Out of nowhere, a harbor patrol boat appears, lights and sirens blaring. "Shit," he sighs.

"Just ignore them," Francis yells as she flashes her middle finger toward them.

The wind has picked up, moving the ship faster than necessary. "Francis, bring them down!" Thorne yells toward his granddaughter.

She starts barking orders at the two teams, who follow her every command perfectly. The spectacle of watching a nearly eighty-year-old human telling lycan and vampires how to lower sails on a three-hundred-year-old pirate ship is something that's not lost on me.

Between the two teams, the sails are lowered, and the ship begins to slow slightly, but not enough. "We're going too fast," I state the obvious.

"Aye, I know," Thorne answers. "We're going to hit the other boats."

The police boat speeds in front of us, slowing down enough to allow the stern of the ship to ram into the back of them, slowing the ship even faster.

"Hide what's left of Bertram," Thorne warns. "They're going to come aboard."

I follow the directions, lifting the powdery remains of my brother and hiding them in the captain's quarters.

The ship slows to nothing several yards from the marina. Everyone on board sighs in relief. Applause echoes from nearby boats, as unsuspecting humans stare in awe at the pirate ship that just entered the port of Charleston.

Just as Thorne suggested, three policemen board the ship, hands on their weapons. "What's the meaning of this?" the shorter of the three shouts toward Thorne.

He moves quickly in front of them with his hands at his sides. "I steered her into the wrong port," he lies. "It was completely my fault." He smiles a smile that can charm just about everyone he meets. "Thank you for your help, officers."

"Where are your papers?"

"I'm not sure," he answers. "However, I will cover any damages that may have occurred."

"Gentlemen," Connor greets the officers. "I'm sure we can work this out."

"Mr. McFadden. I didn't realize you were on board," one of the officers responds.

Connor straightens his now untucked shirt. "This ship is owned by Wolf Tours. I have all the paperwork at my office in the city. I'm afraid I neglected to bring it with me today."

"Yes, sir," the men answer. I'm not sure what kind of fuckery is happening before my eyes, but Connor must have major control of the city and the people who run it.

"Why don't you stop by tomorrow, and I'll give you copies?"

"That will be fine. Thank you, Mr. McFadden," the taller of the three answers before leading them off the deck.

"Did I just witness witchcraft in the flesh?" Luna asks, crossing her arms across her chest.

"No witchcraft." Connor laughs. "It's amazing what a little money and donations will do for an organization."

"Not to state the obvious, but how the hell are we going to get to land? Our ride just left." Francis doesn't look the least bit winded after helping guide the ship into port.

Connor pulls his phone out and is talking with someone within seconds. "My son is coming to get us."

Francis stares at Micah. "Your son is on the ship with us."

"My younger brother, Sam," Micah answers with a smile.

"While we're waiting, we should comb the ship for any clues to where Kragen and Samirah might have gone," Elias announces.

"Aye, but be careful. There could still be someone on board. Kragen's not the sort of man who would leave his ship without protection." Thorne resumes the role of captain quickly. He turns, slipping a hand behind my back. "I'll come with you."

"No, you won't."

"Elsie, you can't be angry at me. That was years ago, and it meant nothing more than sex."

"You're not helping your situation," I retort before storming off, leaving him alone on deck. I slide down the stairs, to the bottom of the ship and the hole where I lived for nearly one hundred years. In all honesty, I don't have a right to be angry, but I am. For all he knew, I was dead. But the thought of him wrapped in Samirah's arms, especially knowing that she was Kragen's lover too, pisses me off.

I clear my mind and continue moving through the seemingly empty ship. Remnants of the five humans I freed are still lying around. A few pieces of clothing, tattered blankets, and empty syringes litter the floor. The smell of death and drugs still fills the air.

I move further through the ship to the crew's quarters. Quarters isn't the correct word. It's more like a large room with hammocks stacked on top of each other. I laugh at the irony of vampires having hammocks to sleep in. Maybe Kragen added them for show. Certainly, no one ever used them for their intended purpose.

A loud crash sounds from the room opposite of me. I freeze, not sure what to expect. "Sorry," Luna's voice echoes.

"Be careful," Micah's deep voice answers. "If there is anything on this ship, they're going to find us."

"There's no one over here," I say, moving next to the two of them.

"Yeah, nothing on this one either. Did you find any clues where Kragen and Samirah may have gone?" Luna asks.

"Nothing. He's not stupid enough to go back to the Outer Banks. He could be anywhere in the world right now."

"I found something," Thorne's deep voice calls from upstairs.

"That sounds like it's coming from the captain's quarters." I run up the stairs with the two lycan on my tail.

We enter, finding everyone else already there. They form a circle around Thorne, who looks like he's holding a bomb.

"Is that...is that a bomb?" Luna asks.

"Aye, I think it is," Thorne answers.

"That son of a bitch." Micah moves in front of Thorne. "I spent a little time in the military. I think I can diffuse it. Hold it still."

Micah looks at every angle of the small blue box, as Thorne holds it close to his body. A series of wires are attached in various spots, giving it a very "made in the basement" type of look.

Several minutes pass before Micah speaks. "I don't think this is real. There's no detonator and no timer."

"What are you saying?" Thorne asks.

"I'm saying that I think this is a dummy bomb."

"What if you're wrong?" I ask.

"Then it's over for the lycan." Micah wraps his fingers around two of the wires attached to the box. "1, 2…"

"Why are we counting?" Francis asks, coming into the room.

"Shh…" the room answers in unison.

"Is that a bomb?"

Micah pulls two of the wires at the same time and squints his eyes. Several minutes pass in silence. "Nope," he answers Francis's question. "Just supposed to look like one."

"I spent several days in this room. That wasn't in here earlier." I look around the group as I speak. "Why would he do that?"

"Maybe he left it behind?" Connor asks.

"Kragen doesn't do anything on accident," I respond. "That was a message."

A deep roar sounds outside the ship. "Sam's here," Micah says, throwing the fake bomb at Luna.

"Shit," she exclaims, trying to catch it.

We make our way outside, finding an exact replica of the boat we took to meet the ship docked alongside us. Instead of the bright neon yellow color of the first one, this one is neon orange and has the words "Wolf Pack" painted on the side.

"You don't even try to hide, do you?" Luna asks as the lycan begin working their way down to the boat.

Connor laughs, following the rest of them overboard.

"Why would Kragen have a fake bomb?" Francis asks as Thorne lifts her into his arms.

"Because he's an asshole," he answers, jumping from the deck of the ship to the boat below. I follow behind, landing beside them. Elias and Abram do the same.

"Howdy, folks," a younger version of Micah says from behind the wheel of the boat. "Looks like you guys could use some help."

"Thanks, bro," Micah answers, still holding the makeshift bomb. "We appreciate this."

"No problem." He nods to the bomb. "Is that thing real?"

"No, dummy bomb," Micah answers as Connor steps to the helm, taking us to shore.

Thirty minutes later, we enter the house that Thorne built. Micah continues to play with the dummy bomb, pulling different pieces off and putting them back in place, while I help Francis gather food for a meal. Anything I can do to keep from being near Thorne right now is great.

"What's going on between the two of you?" Francis asks, mixing the egg salad she just whipped together.

"Nothing," I lie.

She huffs a laugh. "You'd have to be blind to miss

the looks you've been giving him. Does it have something to do with Samirah?"

I sigh, not sure I should have this conversation with her. Thorne is her ancestor. "It does," I finally answer. "They knew each other previously."

"Knew each other, or *knew* each other?"

I smile at the look on her face. "*Knew*".

"You can't expect him to be celibate for two hundred years."

"I know, and I didn't. It's just the fact that it was her, and he didn't tell me. God, I sound like a teenager, don't I?"

"Do you want the truth or a lie?" She smiles. "Why don't you take these into the living room, and I'll make a few more." I follow directions, taking the tray of sandwiches with me.

Micah is sitting on the couch, still enthralled with the dummy bomb, when it cracks into two pieces. Glitter explodes from inside, covering him in sparkles along with a note.

"Guys?" Micah pulls the paper out.

"What's that?" Luna laughs at the glitter covering Micah's torso.

Roses are red,
Violets are blue,
This one wasn't real,
But the next will find you.

"What does that mean?" Francis asks, bringing in the second tray of sandwiches.

Thorne makes eye contact with me with the same thought in his mind.

"There's a bomb in the house!" I scream and scramble toward Francis. Like a well-planned action sequence, Thorne grabs Luna, Elias grabs Connor, and Abram grabs Micah. Each of us uses our bodies as a shield to the mortals in the room.

Seconds later, an explosion rocks my eardrums, sending a low hum through my head. I focus on keeping my weight off of Francis as pieces of the ancient house fall around and on top of me. Her breathing becomes erratic as the weight of the debris is nearly more than I can hold.

"Stay strong," I whisper as the room finally becomes quiet.

"Elsie," a voice calls through my mind. "Elsie!" It takes a few minutes to figure out that's me. I'm Elsie. What the hell happened? Did I pass out? Can vampires pass out? The world around me is black. I can't tell if my eyes are open or closed. I try moving with no luck.

"I'm here," I answer. My voice is weak and muffled.

"I hear you," the voice answers. "We're going to get you out of there."

The sound of wood being thrown and voices yelling brings memories of the bomb to the surface. Oh, my God, Francis. I remember throwing myself on top of her seconds before an explosion.

"Francis?" I whisper to silence with no response.

"Hurry!" I yell to my rescuers. "I don't think she's breathing."

Weight is being lifted off me, allowing a small amount of light into my space. Not enough to see Francis, but enough to tell I'm surrounded by large shards of wood.

"Elsie," the voice repeats.

"Thorne! Hurry, Francis…"

More and more weight is lifted from my back, giving me space to move slightly. Pulling my knees forward, I'm able to create enough space to keep my body over Francis and push upward with my back. The momentum is enough to push the remaining rubble off and provide the air that Francis needs.

Thorne is at my side in an instant. "Is she?" he asks, stopping to listen for her heartbeat. "She's still alive, but barely." I stand, lifting his granddaughter with me. Sirens fill the

air as rescue vehicles of all kinds flood the area, heading our way. "She needs medical attention now," I state the obvious, cradling Francis in my arms.

Her breathing has become worse since being out of the rubble. Each breath is a struggle more than the last. Thorne wipes a tear across his filthy face. He gently takes Francis into his arms and lays her in the safety of the grass surrounding what's left of her home.

"My sweet girl. I'm here with you."

Francis opens one eye. "Captain?"

He nods without speaking. "I'm here." He looks at me, asking a silent question. I nod, giving him permission. "Francis, I can change you. You can live forever."

She winces in pain and opens both eyes slightly. "No," she whispers. "I don't want to live forever in this body." She coughs deeply, spitting blood from her mouth.

"You wouldn't have any more pain. You'd be strong," he argues.

A stray tear streams down her cheek, leaving a path in its wake. "I love you, Grandpa, but it's my time to go." Her eyes shoot in my direction. "Take care of him." Her eyes close as she coughs one more time.

"I will," I reassure her. "I'm sorry, Francis."

She attempts to smile. "I'm not. How many people can say they've met their great-great-great-grand-fathers?"

"Please," Thorne begs.

"No. I love..." Her eyes close as her breathing becomes even more sporadic.

"I love you, too," he cries. Francis takes one last breath until there are no more to take.

He collapses to the ground, with his arms wrapped around his descendant. "Elsie? Is she..."

I nod, taking his hand into mine. "I'm so sorry, Thorne."

A group of EMTs runs toward us with their equip-ment in tow. They move to Francis immediately and begin working on her frail body. For the first time, I look around at what remains of the home Thorne built centuries ago. A few pieces of brick, along with the front steps of the home are the only things left.

Connor and Micah are alive and being cared for by one of the many ambulances on the scene. It takes a few minutes to find Luna, but I finally spot her on a gurney not far from the other lycan. I don't know where Elias and Abram are, but I have no doubt they survived the explosion. We're surrounded by chaos.

Thorne stands with his hands clasped behind his head, as he watches the gurney carrying Francis's body being rolled away. I don't know how to help him.

the funeral

THE NEXT FEW days pass in a flurry of emotion and turmoil. Investigations have been nonstop at the house, ending with a conclusion of a gas leak. Although we know the truth. Thorne has been quiet since Francis's death, and I don't blame him.

Apparently, the Charleston lycan own several homes throughout the city. Connor was kind enough to offer one large enough to house all four vampires, along with Luna.

Sliding into the black dress I purchased especially for the funeral, I find myself staring at the shell of Thorne in front of me. He single-handedly planned her funeral and took care of her estate, refusing to let anyone help.

"Are you going to be okay?" I ask as he slides his cuff links into place. It's a question I've asked dozens of times in the last three days.

"Aye," he answers. The emotion sounding through his voice is the opposite of his words.

Walking behind him, I wrap my arms around his waist. The anger I felt about Samirah has left, replaced by the love I feel for Thorne. "I'm here if you need me."

"Aye, I know." He turns, wrapping his arms around me. "I love you for it." A clock in the hall echoes into the room, chiming its bell eleven times. "It's time to go." He holds his arm toward mine, and together, we exit the stately home and walk toward the location for the ceremony.

Overlooking the Ashley River, a small group of vampires, lycan, and a few unsuspecting humans, gather. The cerulean blue sky is the perfect backdrop to say goodbye to someone we love.

Thorne clears his throat before moving next to the urn holding Francis's ashes. "Thank you all for coming." He pauses. "Francis was a force to be reckoned with. Anyone who had the pleasure of knowing her was truly blessed. She could do everything from making enough food to feed an army to sailing a three-hundred-year-old vessel." A few laughs leave the small crowd.

"She was sharp-tongued, sharp-witted, and loved. This world won't be the same without her in it." He wipes a stray tear. "I wish I could regale this speech with tales of her youth, but I only got to know her recently." He looks around the group. "I think I can speak for everyone here when I say she made more of an impression on me in that short time than many people have made on me through lifetimes."

Thorne picks up Francis's remains. "Thank you, my girl. You were amazing, and I am so proud of you."

Tears fill my eyes with his words. Thorne carries the urn toward the river with the small crowd behind. He opens it, lifts it high into the air, and shakes it, releasing her into the water below.

"You are free," he whispers, wiping tears.

"That was beautiful," Luna says as we work our way back to the home we're borrowing. "Your words were perfect."

"Aye, thank you. She deserved so much more," Thorne answers.

"I think she would've thought that was perfect." I lace my fingers through his as the rest of our small crew walks ahead of us.

Back at the house, the five of us sit, staring at each other. The small talk passing between us is nothing more than banter, ignoring the elephant in the room. Thorne has relaxed and the heavy energy he's carried since Francis's death feels lighter. I'm just about to bring up Kragen when Luna beats me to it.

"So...what are we going to do about the asshat that caused this?" she asks, looking around the room.

"He has to be stopped," Elias adds.

"I've been thinking about everything that's happened." Micah stands, moving across the room toward the fireplace. "Elsie, you thought, hell, we all thought that Kragen wanted to die. That he wanted you to kill him."

"Obviously, that's not true," Luna interrupts. "He's still alive, or dead..." She looks around the room. "Which is it? Alive or dead? I mean, I know you all have a permanent death, but what are you right now?"

Micah pretends she hasn't spoken and continues his thought. "Samirah had to be the one to set the bomb in Francis's house. It only makes logical sense. But why? He got his revenge for the death of Eudora." He nods toward me. "He stole you from Thorne's ship and turned you into a freaking vampire. I would think that would call it even. What is he trying to do? Why try and kill everyone?"

"Because he's a lunatic," I answer. "No matter how much you try to figure out the motives or reasoning behind anything he does, you'll be wrong. Kragen thrives on not following the norm."

"Psychopaths don't follow the rules of society," Thorne adds. "We could spend hours, hell, years trying to figure out why he does and did the things he did. We'll never know."

"He has to be stopped," Abram speaks for the first time.

Thorne stands, moving toward the stairs. "You don't owe me anything. All our debts are paid." He looks between the two vampires. "Thank you for being here, but I won't ask you to stay."

Abram stands. "I think I speak for both of us when I

say we will not rest until Francis's death is avenged. We are here to see this through."

"Me, too." Luna chimes in.

"Yeah, add me to that." Micah joins.

Thorne looks around the room at the makeshift paranormal Avengers. "Thank you, my friends. If you don't mind, I'm going upstairs to change."

I don't wait to be asked. I follow him upstairs to the bedroom we've shared for the past few days. Thorne takes off the sport coat and tie he wore for the funeral. I copy his movement, shedding the semiformal dress and changing into my usual leggings and a T-shirt.

"Elsie, I'm sorry," he says from the edge of the bed.

I move in front of him, resting between his knees. "You don't owe me an apology."

"Aye, I do. If my men hadn't killed Eudora, none of this would've happened. You would have never been taken, and we could have been together the way we were meant to be." He wraps his hands around my waist. "This all happened because of me."

"You can't do that to yourself. None of this is your fault. If anyone is at fault, it's Kragen. He's the one who chose all of this."

"Killing Francis was his way of still punishing me. He's never going to leave you alone, and killing you would be his ultimate revenge. All because of Eudora." He lowers his forehead to mine.

"You're forgetting one important fact. I'm the only one who can kill him."

"I'm not forgetting that. I'm just not putting you in that place again. He took you away from me twice. I won't survive a third time."

"I'm stronger than you think," I remind him.

"I'm not." His voice is no louder than a whisper. "I'm sorry about Samirah," he starts.

I cover his lips with my finger. "That's not important anymore. I'm sorry I was angry. It was dumb."

Thorne places his hands on my cheeks, pulling my face gently toward his. The connection sends chills down my spine. I climb up the tall bed, straddling his hips with mine, and never losing connection with his mouth. Our kisses become deeper, and he pulls me closer.

I rock my body into his, eliciting a deep moan. Enjoying the sound he made, I copy the movement again, this time rubbing myself along his erection.

Thorne slides his hands under the waistband of the thin leggings I'm wearing and grabs my ass firmly, helping me to glide along the hardest part of him.

"Are you okay to do this?" I ask, pulling away slightly.

"I'm more than okay." In one quick motion, he strips off the shirt he's wearing, throwing it in the corner of the room.

I do the same, throwing my T-shirt and leggings nearby. Thorne's pupils dilate as he takes every inch of me in. Unbuckling his belt, I shimmy the dress pants he's wearing down his hips, freeing the part of him I want.

Rubbing my hand along the length of him, he moves in time with my hand. I slide low enough to use both hands. One on his balls, and one on his cock. I work them in tandem while he stares me in the eyes. The look on his face makes me want him even more.

I let go and slide forward, lining us up together. His hands caress my breasts, hitting the perfect spot on my nipples. Slowly, I lower myself onto him until our bodies are flush with each other. Thorne fills me.

I begin moving, lifting myself to the tip and sliding to the base of him. "You feel so good," he sighs.

It doesn't take long before we're moving in unison. I lower my body to his, kissing him deeply as we continue moving. The rhythm of our tongues matches the rhythm of our bodies.

The sensation starts low in my abdomen, covering my body in chill bumps. I sit up, just as the coil spins tightest, and take every inch of him inside. Thorne matches my intensity, and the two of us cry out at the same time.

I collapse on top of him, and it takes a few minutes for both of us to catch our breath. "That was..."

"Yeah." He fills in the blank.

A soft knock on the door draws us back to reality. "I'm sorry to bother you, again... I feel like this is becoming a pattern." Micah's voice echoes through the door. "But Connor's here. He brought someone you need to meet."

"We'll be right down," I answer for both of us.

A few minutes pass before we make our way back downstairs. Connor is standing in the doorway with a larger man not far behind.

"Elsie, this is Christopher St. James, the Alpha of New Orleans."

Thorne moves in front of the Alpha, the top of his head only coming to Christopher's forehead. "Good to see you again, Thorne," he says, shaking Thorne's hand. "Elsie, please call me Topher."

"It's nice to meet you, Topher. What brings the Alpha of New Orleans here?" I ask.

Topher looks down before speaking. "Connor has shared information about what's happened here and the death of your granddaughter. I'm truly sorry."

"Thank you," Thorne whispers. "Me, too."

"I've heard through several of my pack members that Kragen has been spotted off the coast of Louisiana in the Gulf."

"Of course, he has," I spew. "Let me guess, in a pirate ship?"

Topher laughs. "No, in the swamps, and it was more like a canoe."

"Was he alone?" Elias asks.

"There was a woman with him."

"When do we leave?" Abram asks the small group.

"My plane is ready and will hold everyone."

I close my eyes. When will this be over? Will this ever be over?

"Okay," Thorne whispers. He turns toward the small group next to us. "If any—"

"Stop," Luna interrupts. "We've already had this conversation...several times. We're all staying and seeing this through." She moves closer to her Alpha, who wraps a long arm around her shoulders.

"You've done well," Topher praises her, giving her a warm hug. "I have a car waiting out front."

The eight of us load into an extra-large SUV and arrive at the airport not long after. I have no idea what we're going to find when we get there, or what we're walking into. The SUV bypasses the airport and drives straight to the tarmac. Parked in the middle of a smaller runway is a private jet.

"The New Orleans pack must have more money," Connor laughs.

Topher returns the laugh. "That belongs to my wife. She inherited quite a bit of money from her maker."

"Her maker?" I ask, eavesdropping.

"She's a vampire, or at least, she was." Topher laughs awkwardly. "It's a long story."

The jet lifts into the sky, and the group falls mostly quiet. The lycan have been talking quietly, forgetting that we can hear them no matter how softly they speak. Most of their conversations have to do with pack matters and the future of both the Charleston and New Orleans packs.

"Ladies and gentlemen, we are approaching Louis Armstrong International Airport. Please fasten your seatbelts and prepare for landing. The time is five-forty-five, and it's a balmy eighty-four degrees."

"Home, sweet home," Luna says as the plane begins to descend. "Where there's always 100 percent humidity."

Minutes later, the plane is taxiing down the runway and stops in front of a second black SUV. Sticking my head out the door of the plane, I see a strikingly beautiful woman leaning against the driver's side door. Her hair reminds me of fire, and I can sense her otherworldliness instantly. Not only do I feel vampire energy, it's mixed with what I now recognize as lycan energy. Strapped to her chest is a small toddler with the same hair as his mother.

Topher passes me, hurrying down the stairs to greet the woman. They embrace with an almost embarrassing kiss. Luna moves next to me. "That's Amelia and little Edon."

"What is she?"

Luna laughs. "That's up for debate."

The rest of us deboard the plane and follow Topher's footsteps to the SUV.

"Hi, folks," the woman greets us. "I'm Amelia."

We introduce ourselves, each taking a turn to shake her hand, ending with Luna, who gives her a big hug.

"I'm afraid I have some interesting news about your Kragen," she says, bouncing baby Edon. "He's definitely in the swamps, and he's not alone."

"What do you mean?" Thorne asks.

"I mean, he's amassed a small army," she answers.

"You mean he has a new crew," I fill in the blanks.

the big easy

OVER THE YEARS, I've visited New Orleans several times. But until coming here with the Alpha of New Orleans and his wife, I've never experienced the city for what it truly is—a haven for the paranormal.

Walking the streets of the French Quarter is an overwhelming cacophony of smells, sights, and sounds.

"Are you okay over there?" Thorne asks as we pass a large group of tourists. Most of them are drunk and stumbling through the streets.

"It's ten o'clock in the morning. Why the hell are the humans already altered?"

He laughs. "Isn't there a song about it being five o'clock somewhere?"

"Yeah, but that's for the beach, not the downtown area of a major metropolis."

"Welcome to New Orleans," Amelia, our tour guide

for the day, says with a laugh. "You never know what you're going to see."

"Or smell," I add.

"Or smell," she confirms. "That was the hardest part of becoming a vampire...all the smells. I mean I always had a good nose, but when those vampire senses kicked in, ugh."

Amelia's energy is calming, and she's fun to be around. The fact that she's pushing a stroller down Bourbon Street makes me like her even more. There's no doubt that the baby she's pushing is hers, but how did a vampire have a child? I haven't gained enough courage to ask, and honestly, it's none of my business.

"We're here," she says, opening an inconspicuous door next to an empty building.

"Where is here?" Thorne asks, moving in front of me and opening the door wide enough for the stroller to enter.

"This is a speakeasy. It's owned by Erick, one of the older vampires in the city." She pushes the stroller inside with us in tow.

"Is it smart to bring a baby in here?" Thorne asks.

Amelia laughs. "We have much to talk about, my friends."

The dark room immediately comes into focus. The décor reminds me of the quintessential vampire movies from the '60s. Dark wood, meeting dark burgundy carpet, and black velvet seating line the walls of the establishment. "This screams vampire," I say, holding in the laugh that wants to escape.

"Yeah, Erick's a little extra," Amelia says, shoving Edon forward on the thick carpet. She moves to a booth hidden behind a dark curtain. Without asking, she shoves the curtain back, revealing a man dressed in all black. The vampire energy rolls off of him as he stands, ready to reprimand whoever disturbed him.

"Ah, Amelia, my dear." He smiles when he sees her face. "You're looking lovely this fine day." The man wraps long arms around her shoulders, pulling her close and kissing her on each cheek. "What do I owe the pleasure of this visit?"

"These are the people from Charleston I was telling you about." She motions toward me. "Erick Pembroke, may I present Elsbeth Abernathy and Captain Hawthorne Rex?"

Erick reaches for my hand, bringing it to his lips. "Elsbeth. What a charming name," he says with a kiss, lingering longer than he should. He drops my hand gently before clicking his heels together. "Captain." He nods, holding his hand toward Thorne. "It is a pleasure to meet you both. Amelia has spoken highly of both of you."

Erick's words are precise and clear, speaking what's been called the Queen's English. "Thank you," I answer awkwardly.

"Mind if we join you?" Amelia asks, shoving the stroller further toward his booth.

"How rude of me," he answers, moving out of the way. "Please." He motions to the empty seat across from him.

"Elsie and Thorne are looking for Kragen," Amelia announces, as we slide into the empty seat.

Erick leans back at the mention of his name. "For what purpose?" he asks.

"To kill him," I answer simply.

Erick smiles. "I like a woman who's not afraid to speak her mind." He sniffs the air. "Why are you trying to kill your maker? I smell him in your blood." He turns toward Thorne, sniffing deeply. "And you carry the blood of my friend, Viktor."

"Aye," Thorne smiles. "He was my maker."

Amelia and Erick share a look, making me curious about the rest of the story. "I'm curious. What would make you want to kill your maker?" Erick asks, looking straight at me.

I look down, not sure what to say. Because he's an asshole, doesn't feel adequate. "Kragen is responsible for the deaths of tens of thousands of humans over the centuries. He's an evil, cruel man with nothing but hatred in his heart."

Erick nods. "I've known many a vampire over the years that fits into that criterion, but why you?" He slides forward in his seat. His dark eyes pierce into mine.

"Because of what he did to me," I whisper.

"Ah, there we go," Erick answers. "Your eyes are full of pain, and I smell the anger that consumes you."

"It's not just about me," I retort.

"It seems it is," Erick argues.

His words strike a chord. Is it all about me? Have I made this chase with Kragen the ending to a personal vendetta? I move to slide out of the seat. "I apologize for wasting your time."

"Elsie?" Thorne questions.

"Let her go," Erick's words echo through my mind as I exit the dark room back onto the street full of wobbling humans.

"You got some titties you want to show?" an older man with greasy white hair asks, stepping in front of me.

"How much money do you have?" I tease.

The man laughs and hands me half of a torn dollar bill. "It's all I've got left."

I take the torn bill and look him in the eyes. His pupils dilate instantly. "Go home. It's not safe out here. There are creatures that will drink your blood and leave you empty."

The man's eyes come back into focus, and he stares at me blankly. "There are creatures out here. I've got to go home. Are you all right, Miss?"

"Go home," I repeat. The man turns, running down the street toward what I hope is a taxi. Out of the corner of my eye, I catch a glimpse of the sun glimmering off something shiny. It hits me in the eye once more before disappearing from view. What was that?

Moving toward the glimmer, I'm not sure what I expect to find. I reach the spot and meet with a smell I would recognize anywhere...Kragen. The deep smell of sulfur fills my nose.

"Where are you, you bastard?" I whisper into the wind.

I turn, ready to follow the smell, when a dark hand lands on my shoulder. "Don't follow him," a smooth British accent says from behind. The source of the voice steps in front of me, blocking any movement. "If you're going to kill him, you're going to have to be smarter than that," Erick says.

"What happened?" Thorne asks, running to my side.

I sigh, putting my hands on my hips. "Kragen was here."

"Are you sure?" Amelia asks, coming to our side. Baby Edon is laughing and clapping his hands at the speed of their arrival.

"Without a doubt," I answer.

"What makes you think you can kill Kragen?" Erick asks.

"Because of the curse," Thorne answers for me, shifting from foot to foot.

"This is getting better by the minute." Erick crosses long arms across each other, staring at the three of us.

"Who's going to tell me the story?" Amelia copies his movements, staring at the two of us.

"Thorne's granddaughter found information about a curse, or...I don't know if that's even the right word. Anyway, it said that Kragen could only be killed by one of his female children."

"I'm guessing you are his only remaining female creation?" Erick fills in the blank.

"Aye. As far as we know, I'm it."

"And you want him dead because of what he did to you?" he continues.

"Kragen took her in retaliation for the death of his wife, Eudora," Thorne continues the story.

Amelia's eyes grow large. "Eudora, the sea witch?"

"How do you know about her?" I ask, surprised by her knowledge.

"Well, before I was this," she motions down her body, "I was an aspiring Ph.D. student, writing my thesis on mythological beliefs in Europe." She looks between the two of us. "I know. You don't need to say anything." She clears her throat. "I came across information on Eudora in my research. To be honest, I thought they were just stories." She laughs. "I thought the same about vampires and lycan at one time, too. I couldn't have been more wrong," she mutters.

We all stare at her, waiting for more information.

"Oh, sorry. The stories of Eudora are ancient. Like older than time ancient. She was said to hold the power to curse, bless, or murder someone with the blink of an eye." Amelia turns toward Thorne. "You said Kragen took Elsbeth in retaliation for her death? That makes no sense."

"Aye, it does. My men killed Eudora, and Kragen blames me for her death."

Amelia huffs a laugh. "If my research is correct, no mortal man would be able to kill Eudora."

"I saw it with my own eyes," Thorne argues. "She was in the form of a dolphin and appeared sickly. My men captured her in their nets, and I gave the order to end her life."

"I'm sorry, Thorne. There's no way Eudora, the ancient sea witch, would've been caught in a net, let alone appeared as a sick dolphin."

"What are you saying?" I ask our tour guide.

"I'm saying that Kragen is either lying or Eudora tricked him into believing your men killed her."

"Why would she do something like that?" I ask.

Erick shrugs. "Maybe she was bored with him."

"Where does that leave us?" Thorne asks.

"It leaves you with the upper hand," Erick answers. "If Eudora is alive, you can use her to defeat him."

"If Eudora is alive, we're never going to find her," Amelia adds. "She's a sea witch, in case anyone forgot."

"That simply means she will be out to sea," Erick adds wisdom with a hint of sarcasm.

"Do you know where Kragen is?" Amelia asks her friend.

Erick shuffles his feet slightly. "I've heard rumors of him being in the swamps near the coast with a group of vampires he's acquired."

"We've heard those rumors," Amelia continues. "We can't act on rumors."

"Maybe I can help," a young voice says from behind.

All four of us turn quickly toward the source. The smell of sulfur hits me immediately. "Who are you?" I spew. "I smell *him* on you."

The girl staring at us looks no older than me, with a head full of snow-white hair. Bright blue eyes stare at each of us expectantly, and the two dimples on her cheeks indent with her smile. She holds the energy of a vampire along with something else, something very powerful, and nothing I've felt before.

"I'm Marnie." She holds her hand toward me. "It's a pleasure to meet you, Elsbeth Abernathy."

"Who are you to Kragen, Marnie?" Amelia asks.

"He's my father," she answers simply. "Eudora is my mother."

"And here I thought my genealogy was interesting," Amelia says with a smirk.

"You're part lycan and part vampire," Marnie announces, answering my unasked question.

"How'd you know that?" Amelia asks.

Marnie shrugs. "I can tell." She looks down at the red-haired toddler smiling in the stroller. "He's more lycan than vampire."

Amelia pulls the stroller closer. "Don't try anything," she warns.

Marnie scrunches her face. "Why would I try anything?"

"That depends on why you're here," Erick asks.

"I'm here to help."

"Which side?" Thorne steps closer to the adorable teenager.

"Whichever side is against Kragen."

"Nothing personal, dear, but we don't know you from Adam. Are you expecting us to jump at your command and give our full trust to you?" Erick moves closer to the young woman.

"Of course not. However, you might be willing to trust my mother."

Amelia moves even closer. "Eudora?"

"She's requested to meet with you," Marnie continues. She pulls a piece of paper from her hip pocket. "Here is the address." She turns, walking away from us.

"Wait. How do we know we can trust you?" Thorne asks.

"You don't." She smiles, flashing her dimples, and continues walking.

"What was that?" Amelia asks after the girl disappears.

"That was an enigma," Erick answers. "Do you believe she's who she says she is?"

"She carries Kragen's blood. The question is, does

she carry Eudora's blood, as well?" Thorne asks the question we all want to know.

"I have a feeling we'll find out soon," Amelia answers.

****If you enjoyed Elsbeth and Thorne's story, please consider leaving an honest review on Amazon. Your reviews help my books be pushed to more readers. Book 2 is available! Read Now!**

acknowledgments

When I stop and think about where my writing was a year ago, it's hard to believe what it's blossomed into. I have so many people to thank for their continued support and encouragement.

Thank you to Stephanie! Without you, I never would have self-published to start with. Thank you for your continued Alpha reads and for grounding me when I have a crazy idea.

To my son J, who when I mentioned writing a new vampire story based out of Charleston, a city we visited many times in the past, immediately said, Vampire Pirates. And...the story was born.

Madalyn Rae is the pen name for an author who loves telling a story. As a teacher of tiny humans during the day and author by night, she hopes she's able to draw you into her world of fantasy, make-believe, and love, even for a brief moment.

She lives on the Gulf Coast's beautiful white, sandy beaches, with her two loyal yet mildly obnoxious dogs, Whiskey and Tippi. She's the mother of two amazing adult children and a son-in-love.

When not teaching or pretending to write, Madalyn is immersed in the world of music. Whether playing an instrument or singing a song, she is privileged to know that music is the true magic of the universe.

Witches of New Orleans-YA Novella Series

Haunted Hexes-Book 1

Christmas Brew-Book 2

Vampires of Charleston

Voyage of Death and Desire-Book 1

Voyage of Fury and Fate-Book 2

Voyage of Magic and Malice-Book 3

Vampires of New Orleans

Garden of the Past-Prequel Novella

Garden of Secret and Shadow-Book 1

Garden of Mystery and Intrigue -Book 2

Garden of Discovery and Love- Book 3

Ravenwood-Book 4 Spin-off

Garden of Rage and Ruin-Book 5

Morally Gray Novella

Full Moon Christmas

Nipping at Your Nose

Fallen

Lucky

The Elementals

Birth of the Phoenix-Adria's Novella-Prequel

Phoenix of the Sea- Book 1

Guardian of the Sea- Murphy's Novella

Ashes of the Wind- Book 2

Embers of the Flame-Keegan's Novella

Fire of the Sky-Book 3

The Elementals Collection-Box Set

The Elementals Collection